THE HOUSE ON THE SHORE

Roderick Landry, a war artist suffering the after-effects of the trenches, stays for a few weeks at the Cornish hotel where Elvina Simmons lives with her aunts Susie and Tilly. Initially reserved, Roderick eventually warms to Elvina and to life in the sleepy little seaside village. And when, together, they renovate the ruined house on the shore, it seems that their friendship may deepen — to love.

Books by Toni Anders
in the Linford Romance Library:

TONI ANDERS

THE HOUSE ON THE SHORE

Complete and Unabridged

LINFORD
Leicester

First published in Great Britain in 2010

First Linford Edition
published 2010

British Library CIP Data

Anders, Toni.
  The house on the shore. - -
(Linford romance library)
  1. War artists- -Fiction. 2. Dwellings- -
Remodeling- -Fiction. 3. Cornwall
(England: County)- -Fiction. 4. Love
stories. 5. Large type books.
  I. Title II. Series
  823.9′2–dc22

  ISBN 978–1–44480–488–1

Published by
F. A. Thorpe (Publishing)
Anstey, Leicestershire

Set by Words & Graphics Ltd.
Anstey, Leicestershire
Printed and bound in Great Britain by
T. J. International Ltd., Padstow, Cornwall

A Mysterious Guest Arrives At The Hotel

'Who's that? Never seen him around here before. I wonder what he's up to?'

'Don't know. Perhaps he's a walker.'

The two girls perched on the high grassy bank facing the sea looked down at the man striding along the road between them and the beach.

The man, tall and dark-haired, glanced up and seeing them watching him, waved a hand but kept walking.

Elvina waved back but Nancy looked disapproving. 'You shouldn't wave at strangers.'

'Only being polite,' retorted Elvina, 'anyway, he waved first.'

'Ouch, this grass is itchy. Wish we'd brought something to sit on,' Nancy wriggled uncomfortably. Her cotton dress was no protection from the sharp

1

spikes of sea grass.

'Don't think he's a hiker,' mused Elvina. 'Hikers carry rucksacks. Looks like someone out for a walk. It's a mystery. We know everyone in the village.'

'Perhaps he's staying at your hotel.'

Elvina looked interested at the thought. 'Perhaps he is. I'll let you know.' She lay back on the grass and lifted her face to the sun. 'It would be nice if we had someone young and handsome for a change — not like that awful Mr Hale.' She shuddered.

'Is he still pestering you?' her friend asked.

Elvina sat up again. The sun was hot and the sea breezes when she sat upright, were cooling. 'Not pestering me exactly, well, I hope not. But he does seem to get in my way a lot. I wish he'd leave.'

Elvina removed her straw hat, glared at it and put it on the other way round. 'Does it look better this way?'

Nancy studied the hat and made a

face. 'Not much difference,' she said, dismissively. 'A few flowers might improve it. Or cherries. How long is he staying?'

'Not cherries. We used cherries last summer.' After a few seconds she seemed to remember the question. 'How long is who staying?'

'Mr Hale, of course.'

'I don't know. He was ill. He's recuperating, so Small Aunt said.'

'Have you told your aunts that he annoys you?'

'Yes,' said Elvina. 'They think I'm imagining it.'

'Perhaps you are,' said Nancy. She thought that Elvina liked to dramatise her life.

Elvina tossed her head. 'I am not,' she said indignantly. She tightened the large black bow at the back of her long hair.

'If you'd had your hair cut, your hat would stay on better,' said Nancy, complacently stroking her own short locks. She'd had her hair bobbed in a ladies' salon in Penzance the week before. Elvina had gone with her for company, but refused to have her hair cut too.

'I should feel strange with no hair,' she'd protested, 'and my aunts would be cross.'

Now they sat in companionable silence, looking out to sea and watching the heavy rollers pounding on the beach.

'Are you looking forward to the Sunday school treat?' asked Nancy.

'Of course. It's always good fun, especially the races.'

'We're doing the food,' said Nancy. 'Eli is always in a good mood when we have extra orders.'

'Eli? You mean, Mr Bun,' said Elvina with a giggle.

'Don't be rude,' said her friend, with dignity.

Elvina looked at her in amazement. 'You'll be telling me you're sweet on him in a minute,' she said. 'I know he's sweet on you. I've seen the way he looks at you.'

4

Nancy turned her head away and blushed but made no reply. Eli Corey was the village baker and confectioner. Nancy worked part-time in his bakery, serving the customers and occasionally helping to decorate the cakes.

Eli, or Mr Bun as Elvina called him, was small and round with currant eyes and a wide mouth. He was a widower with a fine house at the edge of the village and a smart horse-drawn van for deliveries. He was rumoured to be worth quite a bit of money and ladies on his round frequently offered him a 'sup of hot tea' on a cold morning, or a 'nice cold glass of fresh lemonade' in the summer.

Despite his appearance, Eli Corey was considered quite a catch in the village.

Elvina continued to look at her friend; Nancy continued to look away.

'He's old,' said Elvina. 'He's at least forty-five and you're only nineteen.'

'Can we change the subject?' Nancy's voice was icy. 'You're being stupid.'

Elvina relented. Nancy was more serious than she was. It was a shame to tease her. As if she could ever look at Eli Corey in that way!

She spotted a familiar young man on the road below them. 'Oh look, there's Jack! He's waving. Is it all right if I wave to him?'

Nancy gave her a shove then looked down at her brother. 'What does he want? Come to get me, I suppose.'

'Mam wants you, young Nancy,' Jack called up. He began to climb the grassy bank. 'I'll stay and keep Elf company.'

'No you won't,' said Elvina with a laugh. 'I'm going home too.'

'Can't you stay a few minutes?' pleaded Jack. He'd reached the girls and flung himself down between them. His face shone red like his hair with the exertion of climbing the bank. 'Why do you two always meet up here? It's a hot climb.'

'Keeps people like you away,' retorted Nancy.

'Off you go.' Jack flapped his hand at

his sister. 'Mam's waiting.'

'Oh . . . you . . . ' Nancy made a face at him, ran lightly down the bank and disappeared along the coast road to the village.

Jack lay back on the grass, squinting against the brightness of the sun. 'If you're a good girl, I might take you to the pictures on Saturday,' he said.

'Might you. And what if I'm busy?'

'Then I'll take Annie Kent.'

Elvina sniffed. 'Take Annie Kent, I don't mind. Anyway, I'm going home now.' She stood up.

He jumped up too, agile for such a stocky young man and grabbed her hand. 'I'd rather take you. Please Elvina, I didn't mean to tease you. Will you come?'

She considered. 'Very well. If the aunts can spare me, I'll let you know.'

'I'll walk you home. Come along.'

Hands linked, they climbed down the bank together. Elvina told him about the stranger as they walked. Jack wasn't very interested.

'We're going out on the evening tide,' he said. 'If we get a good catch, I'll buy you a box of chocolates at the Picture Palace.'

Elvina smiled at him warmly. He was a good friend and a skilful fisherman. The chocolates were as good as hers.

'Just watch you don't fall off the boat,' she said as they reached the hotel. Before she could stop him, he'd grabbed her hat and was twirling it round and round on one upraised finger. She snatched it back.

'Are we taking Clay to the pictures with us?' She gave him a teasing smile.

'Don't be daft. Would I be likely to take my brother. It's just you and me.'

Elvina danced up the path, singing to herself.

★ ★ ★

Elvina's aunts were both in the kitchen preparing dinner for their guests. The room was hot and steamy and there was a delicious smell of roasting meat.

The two women smiled fondly at her. Aunt Tilly, known as Tall Aunt, took a pile of tablecloths from a drawer and handed them to her. 'Come along, Miss, tables need laying.'

Elvina took the tablecloths with a grin. Aunt Tilly had a sharp tongue to match her sharp features, but she loved Elvina dearly. She dressed all in grey, but today there was the contrast of a brightly flowered apron.

'Let the girl take her hat off and wash her hands.' Aunt Susie, small and dumpy, known as Small Aunt, was lost in a voluminous white overall. She gave her sister a reproachful look. 'Have a nice afternoon, love?' she asked her niece.

'Mmm. Just chatting to Nancy. And Jack walked me home.'

'Oh yes.' Small Aunt smiled. 'And what will Clay say about that?'

'He can say what he likes,' said Elvina. 'I treat them both the same.'

'I should hope so as they're twins, and you don't favour either.'

'Quite right too,' said Aunt Tilly. 'Our Elvina is too good for the likes of fishermen. Keep them as friends, like when you were young, but nothing more.' Aunt Tilly banged a large saucepan down on the table and began to smash potatoes with a rolling pin.

'Clay isn't a fisherman,' Elvina reminded her.

'You can do better than village lads from the cottages,' said Aunt Tilly.

'Jack wants to take me to the pictures on Saturday. Do you think I can be spared? I'll do extra jobs on Friday night.' She gazed anxiously at her aunts. They looked at each other and smiled.

'I think we could manage without her, don't you, Tilly?' asked Aunt Susie.

Aunt Tilly pursed her lips. 'I don't know. Saturdays are always busy.'

Elvina looked at her with a worried frown. Then Aunt Tilly smiled. 'But I daresay we'll cope.' Elvina gave her a hug and kissed Aunt Susie's soft cheek. 'Thank you, darlings. I'll just go and take off my hat, then I'll be ready.'

She ran upstairs and into her tiny bedroom. The larger rooms in the house were kept for guests but Elvina didn't mind. She liked her neat little white bedroom with its gaily coloured patchwork quilt and its view of the sea.

She poured water from the ewer on the washstand into the flower-patterned china bowl and quickly washed and dried her hands. Then she emptied the water into a bucket under the table.

She studied her reflection in the mirror above the washstand. Her cheeks were pink from sitting in sea breezes all the afternoon. Smoothing back her hair, she made a face at her reflection and ran back downstairs to the kitchen.

There were six tables to be laid for dinner. The hotel was full. Elvina hurried to and fro from kitchen to dining-room with tablecloths, napkins, cutlery and glasses. She placed a small vase of fresh wild flowers on each table. She had collected them that morning from the field behind the hotel.

'How many places shall I lay on table six?' she asked. It had been empty at breakfast.

'Just one,' said Small Aunt. 'We have a new guest — a young man.'

'Right.' Elvina hurried out of the kitchen. As she shook out the cloth and smoothed it over the surface of the table, the figure of the unknown young man on the road near the sea came into her mind. She returned to the kitchen.

'Is he tall and thin with dark hair?'

'What? Who?' Tall Aunt was busy mashing swedes now. 'Oh, the young man. Yes, he is. Why? Have you seen him?' She added a large lump of butter and a shake of pepper to the pan and thumped vigorously. 'I hate swedes with lumps in them.'

'Nancy and I saw him from the top of our bank. He waved to us. Nancy thought he might be staying here. What's he like?

'Very quiet. He was in the war. Looks shell-shocked to me.'

'That sort of experience would take a

lot of getting over,' mused Aunt Susie. 'Poor young man. We must feed him up. I'll find out what sort of cakes he likes.' Aunt Susie thought that food, especially her cakes, was the answer to all problems.

'There — we're ready now,' said Aunt Tilly. 'Go and do the gong, Elvina, there's a love. I can't stand being too near to it.'

Elvina hurried into the hall and picked up the stick with the rubber covered ball on the end. She always loved striking the gong to summon the guests to meals. She shivered with pleasure as the deep booming sound reverberated round the house.

In the kitchen, she put on a gleaming white starched apron, fastened a little lacy band across her forehead and waited for instructions from Aunt Tilly.

'Take these rolls and I'll bring the tureen of soup,' said her aunt. Elvina was amused to see that the strange brightly flowered apron had been replaced with a plain white one. 'Peep and see if they're all ready first,' her aunt instructed.

Elvina went back to the dining-room. The tables were all occupied, all that is, except number six. The unpleasant Mr Hale was unfolding his napkin at table one. The three elderly sisters who twittered their way all through their meal occupied table two.

At table three, the young couple who'd confided to Elvina that they were on their honeymoon, smiled shyly at each other.

Two hearty young ladies who wore thick tweed skirts and heavy boots, and spent their time tramping over the moors, were studying a map at table four. And at table five, a young clergyman and his mother sat in silence.

Table six was unoccupied. Where was the new guest? Elvina turned to go back to the kitchen and report to her aunts, when he hurried down the stairs. She was sure it was the man she'd seen that afternoon. He didn't recognise her, but with a mumbled greeting, went past into the dining-room and to his table.

Elvina placed the basket of hot rolls on the table, and when Aunt Tilly had ladled the soup into bowls, carried it to the guests. It was a job she enjoyed. She smiled at everyone and asked if they'd had an enjoyable day.

Out of politeness she had to speak to Mr Hale, but sometimes he held on to her wrist and she found it hard not to shudder.

'I'd have had a better day if you'd come with me, girlie,' he often said, with a leer. Elvina hated him.

She was pleased to see that tonight he was distracted by the new guest at table six. Perhaps Mr Hale sees him as a rival, she thought.

She carried soup to the young man. 'Good evening, Mr — ' she glanced at the little name card on the table. 'Mr Landry.'

He glanced up and gave her a tight smile. 'Good evening.' He picked up his spoon in a dismissive way. Obviously he didn't want to chat.

Elvina turned away, but not before she'd registered thick dark hair, a pale face and sad grey eyes. Perhaps there'd be a chance to talk to him later.

Elvina was kept busy waiting at tables for the next hour, so she had no time to wonder about Mr Landry. She returned to his table with food several times, but apart from a brief murmur of thanks, he didn't acknowledge her.

* * *

She was free for fifteen minutes while the guests finished their food and left the dining-room. She ran upstairs to her room and opening the window wide, breathed in the fresh sea air. The kitchen and dining-room had been hot and uncomfortable. Elvina loved fresh air.

A stool stood in front of the low window. When she sat on it, it was just the right height to let her lean forward with her arms on the window sill and

16

her chin on her arms. It was her favourite position. She could gaze down at the garden and the beach below and listen to the soft rustle as the waves drew small stones backwards and flung them onto the sand.

Sometimes, in the winter, there was a wild storm. She still liked to sit at the open window and watch the waves galloping towards the beach and crashing onto the shore.

Now she sat and wondered about Mr Landry. What was his first name? Probably not something ordinary like Jack or Johnny, the names of Nancy's brothers. Sebastian? Julian? Alexander? She thought of the heroes of her favourite books and films.

He was very tall and would be quite good-looking if he wasn't so thin. If he stayed long enough, Aunt Susie would fatten him up. Elvina smiled at the thought.

Below the window, in the garden, she saw the two girl hikers. They'd finished dinner and were setting off for an evening walk. They were slim too, but no amount of Small Aunt's fancy cakes would plump out their figures — they'd walk off the extra pounds in no time.

Reluctantly, she left the window and went slowly downstairs. Mr Landry was just leaving the dining-room. He nodded to her, stood aside for her to pass then hurried upstairs.

What an old grouch, she thought. Can't even smile. Deliberately, she began to sing and execute a few dance steps round the tables as she collected the condiment sets.

'You sound happy.'

Elvina spun round. It was the young clergyman. 'My mother left her shawl. I've come back for it.'

She smiled at him, went over to their table and picked up the shawl from the back of the chair. He smiled back. He was a very pleasant young man.

'I'm usually happy,' she confessed. 'I love to sing and dance. Oh, perhaps I shouldn't admit that.'

'Why? Do you think God doesn't

approve of singing and dancing?'

'Well . . . ' Elvina wasn't sure how to answer. Then she asked, 'Do you like dancing?'

'I do, but there's not much opportunity.' She thought he looked rather sad.

'Alfred, did you find my shawl?' The voice from the stairs was sharp and he started guiltily. 'Oh dear, there's Mother. I must go.' He gave Elvina a shy smile and hurried from the room.

Elvina sighed. Why can't people just be happy? She began to load dirty dishes onto a tray and carried them into the dish-cluttered kitchen. Aunt Susie was at the sink, up to her elbows in soapsuds. Aunt Tilly, who had been drying dishes, handed her tea towel to Elvina and began to put away the piles of plates and soup bowls.

'I was wondering what Mr Landry's first name was,' Elvina said to Aunt Susie. She tried to sound as if the question was of no importance.

Aunt Susie gave her a sharp look. 'It's Roderick. Why do you want to know?'

'No special reason. But he's such a misery, I wondered if he had a miserable sort of name.'

Aunt Tilly slammed the cupboard door. 'Don't be too quick to form opinions of people, young lady. Mr Landry has been in the war. He's seen and heard things we can't imagine. Just be thankful you spent the war peacefully at home in Cornwall and not in mud-filled trenches. People like him died to keep you safe.'

Elvina flushed. She felt hurt. She hadn't meant to criticise Mr Landry. It must have been dreadful to be a soldier and leave your home to fight in a foreign land. She'd make a special effort to be kind to him when she met him again.

'How long is he staying with us?'

He hasn't decided but he thinks it might be a long stay,' answered Small Aunt. 'There, all done.' She dried her hands and arms and carefully rubbed in some of the cream Elvina had bought her as a birthday present. She sniffed appreciatively. 'This cream does smell nice. Are you going out this evening, dear?'

Elvina considered. 'I should get on with the blue dress I started last week. I feel as if it will never be finished.' She looked towards the open door. 'But it's such a lovely evening, it's a shame to stay indoors.'

Aunt Susie removed her overall and fetched a hat from the cupboard in the corner. She put it on, staring critically at her reflection in the small mirror on the door. 'I really don't like this hat. I don't know why I don't get a new one.'

'Where are you going?' asked Elvina.

'Just down the hill. I promised Mrs Jeavons I'd have a cup of tea with her and hear all about her new grandchild. I'll be back in good time for supper.'

★ ★ ★

When Aunt Susie had gone, and Aunt Tilly was seated in her favourite armchair with her feet on a stool and a pile of darning in her lap, Elvina wandered out into the garden. It was kept for the visitors, but if they were all out the family could use it. She made her way to the old swing under the apple tree. This was one of her favourite parts of the garden. She began to swing lazily to and fro.

The swing had been put up for her sixteen years ago when, as a frightened little girl of three, she had come to live with Aunt Tilly and Aunt Susie. They were her father's sisters and her only relatives and when first her father, then her mother, had died of influenza, the aunts had rallied round.

It could not have been easy for them, she realised now. They were spinsters, settled in their ways, and the arrival of a small child must have disrupted their lives. But they knew their duty and didn't hesitate to offer a home in their hotel to their small orphaned niece.

For nights she had cried herself to sleep, one night in Aunt Tilly's bed, the next in Aunt Susie's. They had been patient and loving and gradually, the frightened little girl had settled down and begun to enjoy life in the tiny seaside village of Polrame.

And now it's my home, she thought, and I can't imagine living anywhere else.

She became aware that someone had come into the garden and was walking down the path at the side of the fruit trees. She peeped out. It was Roderick Landry. She slipped down from the swing.

'Good evening, Mr Landry.'

He stopped and looked round. 'Oh, good evening, Miss . . . er . . . '

'Simmons,' she said. 'Elvina Simmons. My aunts own Shellhaven House.' She fell into step beside him. 'Isn't it a beautiful evening.'

He sighed. 'Yes. Beautiful.'

'We have a little terrace at the end of the garden,' she said. 'It overlooks the sea. Sometimes guests sit there for afternoon tea or for a drink in the evening.'

He made no reply.

They reached the end of the garden. She turned to a gap in the wall where three steps led down to a terrace.

'Down here,' she called, turning to see that he was following. He made his way through the tables and chairs and went to lean on the wall looking out to sea. He ignored Elvina.

She looked at his back, at first resentfully, then, remembering that she meant to be friendly, with compassion.

'I could bring you some coffee or a drink,' she suggested. 'It's very nice sitting here and watching the daylight go and the moon come up.'

He sighed and turned towards her. 'Thank you, but no. I'm going for a walk. I'll see you at breakfast. Goodnight.' In a few seconds, he was gone.

'Well!' said Elvina, out loud. 'So much for trying to be friendly to you, Mr Stuck-up Landry.'

She stood for a few moments wondering what to do. It really was a lovely evening, the breezes off the sea

24

were light and fresh, wafting the scent of the shrubs and flowers around the terrace towards her. She didn't want to go back indoors.

Strangely, she felt slighted at being so easily dismissed by Mr Landry. She wasn't unattractive. Surely a soldier who'd spent so much time away from feminine company would welcome conversation with a friendly young woman.

Slowly she walked back up the garden path. Perhaps Nancy would like to come for a walk. But if she went down the hill, Mr Landry might think she was following him. She went back to the terrace, opened a little wooden gate in the corner and made her way down a narrow, winding cliff path to the beach.

She hurried across the sand to a little path which led between bathing huts to a lane. Halfway along was Nancy's cottage. Nancy was in the garden, playing with her puppy, Skipper.

Elvina sat down on an old bench next

to her friend. Skipper, his tail wagging violently, dropped a ball at her feet. She threw it and he raced after it but was back in a moment waiting hopefully for her to throw it again. She stood up.

'Come on. Let's take Skipper for a run on the beach.'

'He is staying with us,' she said, as she hurled the ball further for the little terrier.

'Who? The stranger?'

Elvina nodded.

'What's he like? Have you talked to him?' Nancy was excited. A new man was a welcome addition to their little village.

'I've tried.' Elvina threw the ball again. 'I decided to be kind and friendly to him.'

'Why?'

'He's just come back from the war. He seems sad.'

Nancy looked thoughtful. 'So you decided to be kind to him. What happened?'

'He practically ignored me. I offered

to bring him a drink on the terrace — I would have stayed and talked to him if he was lonely.'

'And?'

'He said he was going for a walk and disappeared.'

'Perhaps he's shy. Try again tomorrow.'

'I can't be bothered. And I'm not running after any man — no matter how attractive.'

'So he's attractive.' Nancy looked pleased. 'Perhaps I'll come up to see you tomorrow after breakfast. He might like to chat to me.'

'Don't bother,' said Elvina. 'He's not worth it. If he wants to be a misery, he can be a misery by himself. Come on, Skipper.' She began to run back towards Nancy's cottage, the little dog barking excitedly at her heels.

Half an hour later, she was strolling back up the hill. There was no sign of Roderick Landry. She considered what she had said to Nancy, 'no matter how attractive.' So it had registered that he was attractive, despite her annoyance with him.

Perhaps she'd give him another chance. In the morning, she'd try to have a conversation again. If she failed, well, Nancy could try her luck.

Elvina And Roderick Become Friends

Roderick Landry had not arrived in the dining-room when Elvina began taking breakfast orders the next day. She was in the kitchen collecting plates of bacon and eggs for the early risers when he took his place at table six. She re-entered the room and her heart beat faster when she glanced at his table. He certainly was attractive. If only his mood this morning matched his looks.

'Good morning, Mr Landry,' she said brightly. 'What would you like for breakfast?'

He looked up expectantly.

'We have porridge, kippers, bacon and eggs . . . '

'Bacon and eggs will be fine,' he cut in. 'And a pot of tea.' He opened the book he had brought down with him.

29

'Did you enjoy your walk last night?' she asked.

He looked up slowly from the book. 'Walk? Oh yes, thank you, it was most pleasant.' He turned to the book again.

Well I've tried, Elvina told herself. He just doesn't want to talk to me. She went out of the room.

Nancy's young brother, Johnny, was at the kitchen door with a little basket on wheels.

'Take the washing, dear,' said Aunt Tilly. 'His money is on the shelf behind you.'

Elvina picked up the little pile of pennies and went to the door. Johnny collected dirty washing from the hotel at the beginning of each week and delivered it to a cottage at the far side of the village. There, two elderly ladies washed it in great coppers and dried it on lines stretched between trees in their garden. When it had been ironed, they packed it carefully in the little trolley and Johnny took it back to the aunts.

Elvina lifted the clean washing

carefully from the basket and handed Johnny the pennies. He gave her a cheeky grin and touched the wide peak of his cap.

'Mam says I can keep a penny for myself,' he confided. 'I'm going to buy two gobstoppers. Would you like first suck?'

Elvina shuddered. 'No thank you. I stopped sucking gobstoppers years ago.' She was about to close the door when a thought struck her. 'Would you like something to eat?'

'Yes please,' said Johnny promptly. He was always hungry.

'Wait here.' Elvina put the gleaming white clothes carefully on the armchair in the corner. Then she sandwiched some cold bacon between two left over slices of toast and took them to the door.

The boy's eyes shone. 'Thanks very much. You're a brick, Elf.'

'When you've finished in the dining-room, will you make a start on changing the beds?' asked Aunt Susie.

'Start with Mr Hale's room.'

Elvina made a face. 'Not Mr Hale's, please Aunt. Couldn't I do the young ladies? You could do Mr Hale when you've finished here.'

'Whatever is the matter with you?' asked her aunt.

'I don't like Mr Hale. He . . . he looks at me. And sometimes he grabs my hand.'

'Don't be silly, he's just being friendly. Why, he's old enough to be your father. Why must you make a drama out of everything, Elvina? Anyway, he's in the garden smoking his pipe. If you hurry, you can finish his room before he comes in.'

Elvina quickly cleared the dishes from the now empty dining-room, grabbed the clean washing and flew upstairs. She put the sheets and pillow cases on a table on the landing and took two of each into Mr Hale's room.

She glanced out of the window. The man was sitting on a bench, puffing away at his pipe. Good. Please let him stay there for another ten minutes.

She whipped the dirty sheets off the bed, replaced the bottom one and put clean, crisp pillow cases on the pillows. She was shaking out the top sheet when the door opened. She spun round. Mr Hale was watching from the doorway.

'Well, well, well. What have we here? A little maid, morning fresh,' he leered.

Elvina quickly tucked in the sheet, added blankets and a bedspread and scooping up the dirty bedding, walked determinedly towards the door. Mr Hale stayed in the door way.

'May I pass. Please, Mr Hale?' Elvina willed her voice to be steady.

'What's the hurry? Stay for a few minutes. I'd like to talk to you.'

'I have jobs to do,' she said. 'Please let me pass.' She felt a firm grip on her wrist.

'I just want to talk to you. It would pay you to be nice to me. I could take you away from this backwater. Pretty girl like you doesn't want to spend her time skivvying. I could take you to London — even marry you. Come on — give me a kiss as a token of your interest.'

Elvina tugged her arm free. He grabbed her shoulders and attempted to kiss her. She turned her head away in revulsion and called out in panic.

Her aunts were busy in the kitchen and couldn't hear her. Desperately, she shouted more loudly, 'Help, someone, please!'

'Be quiet, you silly little thing,' hissed Mr Hale.

'What do you think you're doing?' came an irate voice from the landing. Roderick Landry pulled Mr Hale round to face him and thrust him up against the wall.

Elvina ducked past them and flew down the stairs. She could hear male voices arguing above as she dropped the dirty sheets near the kitchen door and raced out into the garden.

She felt mortified. Roderick Landry had rescued her but what if he thought she'd encouraged Mr Hale?

In a few minutes, Roderick joined her. He stood several feet away and lit a cigarette. 'Are you all right?'

He offered her a cigarette but she shook her head. 'I'm all right. And thank you for coming to my rescue.'

'Has he pestered you before?'

'Yes,' she said quietly. 'I try to keep out of his way.'

'You should tell your aunts.'

'If I did they'd send him away. They can't afford to do that. He has the most expensive room and he's long term. I can generally cope with him. But he was worse than usual this morning.' Perhaps because you are here, she thought. He sees you as a rival.

'I think you should tell your aunts.'

Elvina shook her head. Roderick continued to smoke and said nothing.

'I must go back in,' she said at last. 'There's lots to do in the mornings.'

'What about the afternoons? Are you busy then?'

Elvina felt her mouth go dry. Was he

going to suggest that they . . . ?

'I noticed some tennis courts near the sea when I was walking last night. Do you play?'

'I'm not very good,' she admitted.

'Are you free this afternoon?'

'I usually have the afternoons off. Yes, I'm free this afternoon.'

'Would you give me a game?' He ground out his cigarette and looked at her. 'We could have tea or an ice. I believe there's a café.'

There was still a severe expression on his face as if smiling was something he'd forgotten how to do. But it was an invitation. Elvina determined to accept.

'I'm not very good,' she repeated.

'Neither am I. I was once, but I haven't been able to play for years. So we should be an equal match.'

'Elvina! Elvina!' Aunt Tilly appeared in the doorway. 'Excuse me, Mr Landry, but Elvina has several things to do this morning.' She disappeared.

Elvina gave him an apologetic smile. 'I really must go. I'll see you at two o'clock if that will do.'

He nodded. 'I'll be ready.'

* * *

The tennis courts had been built some years ago near the beach, just a short walk from the centre of the village. There was a small clubhouse and above, a café open to the public,

'Game first or refreshments first?' asked Roderick as they approached the courts.

'Game first,' she said, 'if there's a court free.'

There was, and leaving their belongings in the clubhouse, they went out into the sunshine.

Elvina watched Roderick as he strolled to the opposite end of the court. Tennis whites suited his dark hair and his long legs.

She felt quite satisfied with her own appearance. Her white cotton dress was embroidered at the neck and on the belt with tiny silver flowers. She wore white stockings and comfortable shoes. She was afraid she wouldn't give him much of a game but hoped her appearance, as she played, would make up for it.

They played for an hour. Elvina acquitted herself quite well. Of course he beat her, but not ignominiously so.

'Well played, partner,' Roderick said, generously. 'I think that had better be enough for today. It's very hot and I haven't played for ages. I need to get myself back into it gradually.'

'It's my first game this year,' she admitted. 'I agree we should stop now.'

They retrieved their belongings from the clubhouse and made their way to the steps which led up to the café.

Two girls were coming towards them down the steps. Elvina smiled at the wide-eyed surprise of the girl in front.

'Elvina,' said Nancy, 'what are you . . . ?'

Elvina turned to Roderick who was right behind her. 'This is Roderick Landry,' she said to Nancy. 'He's

38

staying at the hotel. This is my best friend, Miss Nancy Perrans and Miss Annie Kent, another friend.'

Elvina could see that Nancy was bursting with questions, but now was not the time to ask them. The girls smiled at Roderick who bowed his head to them, gravely.

'Won't you join us for tea?' he asked politely.

Nancy looked as if it was the one thing she wanted to do, but to Elvina's relief, she refused.

'We've booked the court for four o'clock,' Nancy said regretfully.

Roderick bowed his head again. 'A pity. Perhaps another time. We've had our game. Now we're going up to the café.'

They said their goodbyes and as Nancy passed Elvina she whispered, 'I'll be down to see you this evening.'

Roderick found a vacant table near a window overlooking the sea. The café was crowded. Elvina gave a quick look around to see if there was anyone there whom she knew. She rather liked the idea of being seen having tea with a mystery man but she couldn't spot anyone who would be interested.

A waitress appeared and Roderick ordered tea and cakes.

'Are you hungry?' he asked. 'Has playing tennis given you an appetite?'

'No, I'm not really very hungry. But I'm afraid I do like cakes.'

'Me too,' he said and smiled at the surprise on her face. 'Aren't men supposed to like cakes?'

'Oh yes. My Small Aunt will be very pleased. She plans to make you some of her special cakes.'

'She plans to make them for me. Why?'

Elvina grinned. 'She thinks you need feeding up.'

He was silent for a few minutes then he said, 'That's very kind of her. I must admit I've been on extremely unappetising food for a few years. The cooks did their best but conditions in the trenches didn't lend themselves to haute cuisine. I lost a lot of weight.'

The cakes arrived, iced and cream filled. Elvina pushed the plate towards him. 'Come on. Make a start now,' she urged. 'I'll pour the tea.'

'Your friends look very jolly,' he said, after a while.

Elvina considered. 'Annie isn't a close friend,' she said, 'but Nancy has been my best friend since we started school together. We're more like sisters.'

'You haven't any real sisters?'

'No. Nor brothers. My parents died when I was tiny. I was their only child.'

'So you live with your aunts?'

She smiled. 'Yes, and they're darlings. They spoil me dreadfully. So I try to help them as much as I can.'

He passed the plate of cakes to her and took another himself. 'I should have liked a sister. I had a brother, Seymour. He was killed in the war.'

'Oh. I'm so sorry.' Her face fell. 'But you have parents?'

'Yes. They live in a small village in the Midlands.'

She wanted to ask what he was doing

in Cornwall but felt that would be too inquisitive. Instead, she went back to the topic of her best friend.

'Nancy works part-time in the village bakery,' she said, 'in the shop. Sometimes she decorates cakes. She's very good at that — very artistic. Perhaps she decorated these.' She studied her iced cake.

He smiled at her and passed his cup for more tea. Elvina poured them each another cup then sat frowning.

'Is anything wrong?' he asked.

'I was just thinking about Mr Bun.'

'Mr Bun?'

'Nancy's employer. That's what we call him but his name's really Mr Corey — Eli Corey.'

'Why did you frown? Don't you like him?'

'He's very nice,' she said after a moment's thought. 'But he's old. Far too old for Nancy.'

Roderick looked startled. 'Far too old for Nancy. Are they going to be married then?'

Elvina burst into peals of laughter. 'Married! Goodness me, no. It's just that he seems very fond of Nancy. I don't like it.'

'Would he be a bad match?'

'He'd be a very good match for someone nearer his age. But he's forty-five! Forty-five,' she repeated. 'Nancy's only nineteen.'

Roderick looked at her thoughtfully. 'Girls often marry men older than themselves,' he remarked.

'But not that much older. Anyway, she's not going to marry him, so he can stop looking at her in that . . . that . . . soppy way.'

'Poor Mr Bun,' said Roderick, smiling. 'He has upset you.'

'I'm sorry,' said Elvina. 'I shouldn't go on like that to you. You don't know them. It's just that . . . I want the best for Nancy. And,' she looked up shyly at him, 'you're very easy to talk to.'

'I'm flattered,' he said, gravely. 'But perhaps you're worrying unnecessarily.

Perhaps her employer just thinks she's a good worker.'

'Mmm. Perhaps that's it.' Elvina looked around. Many of the people at adjoining tables had left. 'Do you have the time? Perhaps we should be going.'

'It's half-past four.'

Elvina gathered up her bag and racquet. 'Would you mind if I went back now? I have to help prepare dinner.'

'I'm going back too. I have a book I want to read. Perhaps I'll go down to your little terrace.'

Elvina beamed with pleasure. 'Please do. It's very pleasant there.'

He insisted on carrying her racquet and they strolled back to the hotel almost in silence, lost in their own thoughts.

How wrong can you be about a person, thought Elvina. She'd called him Mr Stuck-up Landry and a misery. She was wrong. He was kind and thoughtful and she'd really enjoyed the afternoon with him. She dared to hope

44

he might ask her out again.

He was looking at her as they walked. 'You're miles away,' he said. 'I asked whether we could have a game another afternoon?'

'That would be lovely.' So wishes can come true, she told herself, happily.

They'd reached the hotel. Roderick handed her her racquet. 'Thank you again for a delightful afternoon,' he said. He entered the front door and Elvina slipped round to the kitchen door.

'Well! No need to ask if you've enjoyed yourself,' said Aunt Tilly.

Elvina gave her aunts a wide smile. 'Roderick and I have had a wonderful afternoon,' she said.

'My, my, Roderick is it now?' said Aunt Susie. 'So you've changed your mind about him. I'm very glad. You should never judge a book by its cover, as they say.'

'Well this book has a very interesting story in it,' said Elvina pertly. 'I'll go up and change then I'll be ready to help.'

* * *

During dinner, Roderick gave her a special smile, but they didn't speak except to discuss his meal.

But Elvina was happy. It would not have been suitable to have a long conversation; she was content that he was there and had acknowledged her.

Mr Hale noticed the smile and glared across the room. Elvina felt nervous as she carried a bowl of soup to his table. Then she scolded herself. What did she think he was going to do — shout at her or throw the soup?

She said a quick, 'Good evening, Mr Hale,' and moved away before he could speak.

In the kitchen, when the meal was over, the aunts were looking solemn.

'Mr Hale has told us that he intends to leave at the end of the week,' said Aunt Tilly.

Elvina paused in the act of lifting a pile of soup plates into the cupboard. She looked up but said nothing.

There was a pause, then Aunt Tilly said, 'Perhaps you'd better tell us what happened this morning. Obviously something did, because there was a pile of dirty bedding on the floor and you were in the garden with Mr Landry.'

'We didn't intend to ask you,' said Aunt Susie, 'but we think it concerns Mr Hale, so we need to know.'

Elvina closed the cupboard door slowly. 'I've told you before that he pesters me,' she said. 'This morning when I was in his room, he pushed me up against the wall and tried to kiss me. It was horrible.' She shuddered and the two older women exchanged glances.

'I called out,' Elvina went on. 'You didn't hear me but Mr Landry did. He came in and grabbed Mr Hale and . . . well, I don't know what happened then because I dashed downstairs and into the garden.'

Aunt Susie came across and put her arms round the girl. 'Thank you for telling us,' she said. 'Of course he'll

47

have to go. We shan't try to persuade him to stay.'

'But you'll lose the money for his room,' said Elvina.

'That can't be helped,' said Tall Aunt. 'He's obviously an unpleasant man. We'll soon get someone else, I'm sure.'

'If you and Mr Landry are friends now,' smiled Aunt Susie, 'something good has come out of it.'

'I'm very sorry,' said Elvina, 'but it really wasn't my fault.'

'Don't think any more about it,' said Aunt Susie.

There was a knock at the kitchen door. It opened and Nancy came in. 'Oh, I'm sorry,' she said. 'Am I too early? You haven't finished your chores.'

'We've been having a bit of a discussion,' said Aunt Tilly. 'Elvina will be finished soon.'

'Would you like some trifle?' asked Aunt Susie. 'There was quite a bit left over this evening.'

Leaving Nancy sitting by the kitchen range with her bowl of trifle, Elvina went upstairs to change. She glanced from the window and saw Roderick Landry walking down the path to the sea. So he was off on another of his solitary walks. For one moment, she wondered why he hadn't asked her to go with him.

But why should he do that? One game of tennis doesn't mean that we have to do everything else together. But she couldn't help a feeling of disappointment.

She slipped into a skirt and soft jumper. It was a lovely evening again and she and Nancy would go for a walk or perhaps sit on the terrace. Nancy would want to know all about the afternoon.

★ ★ ★

Nancy chose the terrace. This time she had left Skipper at home so they had no reason to run along the beach.

'Go on then, tell me all about it,' she said as they settled themselves.

'All about what?'

'Don't play the innocent. Yesterday, Mr Landry was stuck-up and you weren't going to bother with him. Today, he's Roderick and you're playing tennis and eating cakes together.'

'I have the dreadful Mr Hale to thank for that,' Elvina replied. 'By the way, he's leaving at the end of the week.'

'Tell me the whole story.' Nancy settled herself with her feet on an adjoining chair, prepared to enjoy the tale.

Elvina left nothing out. Nancy listened without interrupting. When her friend had finished, she let out a long sigh.

'It's like a story in a film,' she said. 'The villain brings the young lovers together.'

'We're not young lovers,' Elvina protested. 'You and your films.'

'Well he certainly seems interested in you.'

'He doesn't know anyone else down here,' said Elvina. 'He just fancied a game of tennis. It doesn't mean anything.' But as she said it, she knew she wanted it to mean something. She was attracted to Roderick Landry. She would be sad to be just a momentary diversion to him.

'So where is he now?'

'Gone for a walk.'

'On his own?' Nancy gave her a sly smile.

'Of course on his own. Look, forget about my affairs. Why did you come over this evening? Was it just to ask nosy questions?' She smiled to soften the comment.

Nancy became serious. 'I've come to ask if I can borrow your red cape.'

'The velvet one? Of course you can. Are you going somewhere special?'

Nancy flushed and looked away from her friend to stare out across the sea. 'I'm being taken out to dinner.'

Elvina looked at her with respect. 'Taken out to dinner! Very grand. Have you met a millionaire or a wealthy film star?'

'Mr Corey is taking me,' said Nancy. 'We're going to The Smugglers' Rest.' At last she turned her head to look defiantly at Elvina, daring her to make a flippant comment.

There was silence between them for a few minutes then Elvina said, 'Of course you can borrow my cape. Come upstairs.'

She lifted the deep red velvet cape from her wardrobe and laid it on the bed. 'What dress shall you wear with it?'

'The white one that Aunt Olive bought me,' said Nancy. 'It's the only suitable thing I have. I've been waiting to go somewhere nice to wear it.'

Nancy's Aunt Olive had done very well for herself and lived in London. Nancy was her god-daughter and every so often, she remembered this fact and sent Nancy an exciting present.

Last year it was a white silk dress with a beaded bodice and little fly-away sleeves. Both girls admired it but neither could imagine when Nancy would wear it. It hung, shrouded in tissue paper in her wardrobe, waiting for the right occasion.

That occasion had come and with Elvina's beautiful red cape, Nancy would look suitably elegant.

But for Eli Corey, Elvina thought with dismay. Why couldn't Nancy have met a handsome stranger? Someone like Roderick Landry. But she can't have him, she thought hastily. He's mine.

Aware of her friend's disapproval, but with a certain pride, Nancy began to tell her about Eli Corey's invitation.

'We'd just locked up the shop, when he suddenly said, 'Would you let me take you out to dinner one night, Miss Nancy?' I was too surprised to say anything at first, then he said, 'We could go to The Smugglers' Rest if you like. The food is wonderful.' Well, what would you have said?'

Elvina thought of the little baker with his currant bun face and currant bun eyes. She thought she would have refused. Nancy looked at her friend's face and read the answer there.

'It's all right for you, Elf,' she burst out. 'You've got more confidence than me. And you're prettier. You never have any trouble getting boys interested in you. I'm different. I can't joke and tease like you do. No,' she held up a hand. 'Let me say it now I've started. This might be just a single invitation or it might lead to something else.'

'You don't mean — marriage?'

'If Eli Corey wants to marry me, I should think very seriously about it,' said Nancy. 'He's kind and has a lovely house — and he seems to have plenty of money. These things are important.'

'But Nan,' Elvina's voice was coaxing. 'He's forty-five, you're nineteen.'

'I don't care. That doesn't matter.' Nancy stood up and carefully folded the red cape. She gave a little laugh. 'Aren't we jumping ahead rather fast? I'm going out to dinner, that's all.'

Elvina found a large bag and slid the cape inside. She decided not to say any more. She didn't want to spoil Nancy's treat.

'When are you going to The Smugglers' Rest?'

'Tomorrow. He's calling for me at seven.'

'In the horse-drawn bread van?' asked Elvina with a little chuckle.

'As you know quite well, Mr Corey recently bought a very smart black roadster car,' said Nancy, with dignity. 'We shall go in that. If you say any more, Elvina Simmons, I shall think you're jealous!' She picked up the bag and swept out of the room.

Elvina Learns Of Roderick's Past

Two days later, Elvina couldn't resist calling in at the bakery on the pretext of choosing some cakes for tea. She wanted to see Nancy and discover if there was anything different about her. Opening the shop door, she was enveloped in the warm smell of baking bread, the sharpness of ginger and lemon and the sweet scent of icing sugar.

'I thought your Aunt Susie made cakes for the guests,' Nancy said, giving Elvina a suspicious look.

'Oh, she does,' Elvina said hastily. 'These aren't for guests, these are a little treat for the aunts and me.'

Nancy looked pleased. 'These are very good,' she said. 'They have a coffee flavour. I decorated them myself. The icing is chocolate flavoured. It's called mocha when you use coffee and chocolate together.'

'Mocha.' Elvina looked impressed. 'I'll have three of those and three cream buns.'

She watched as Nancy carefully placed the cakes in a bag and put them in the marketing basket Elvina was carrying. Elvina handed over the money and turned to leave the shop.

In the doorway she turned back. 'Did you have a nice time last night?' she asked, trying to show only a casual interest.

'Lovely! The food was scrumptious. We had roast chicken. We shall probably go again.'

Elvina looked at her friend. She had a dreadful feeling that Nancy was drifting out of her reach. 'Shall I see you this evening?' she asked.

'No. I've promised to help Mother turn up her new dress. But I'll see you soon.'

Elvina went thoughtfully out into the

sunshine. Was Nancy going to change completely? She wandered down the street towards the tiny harbour. A familiar figure was leaning on the sea wall staring out across the shimmering waves. Roderick! Elvina quickened her step.

He didn't look up as she came to stand near him. Shyly, she touched his sleeve.

'You seem miles away.'

He turned slowly and met her eyes. 'Not so very far away,' he said, quietly.

They stood in silence for a few minutes. Below them, in the harbour, the fishing boats bobbed on the waves and huge grey and white gulls jumped from one boat to another.

'You . . . you don't look very happy today,' she ventured softly.

Roderick passed a hand over his face. 'Memories,' he said quietly. 'I can't get them out of my mind.'

Elvina stood silently at his side, afraid to speak, afraid to say the wrong thing.

'I was a war artist,' said Roderick. 'I

travelled about behind the lines, often very near the front line, recording scenes and impressions of the war.'

Elvina stood, as still as a statue, her wide eyes fixed on his face as he gazed out to sea. She had never heard of a war artist. To her, artists painted beautiful pictures such as the country scenes on the walls of the hotel.

'I knew France years ago,' Roderick went on, quietly. 'It was a beautiful country with peaceful, golden countryside. The war turned the countryside into a muddy, trampled battlefield.

'Sometimes, at night, the trenches looked strange and mysterious lit by lamps and moonlight. I often painted at night. At least then, when the guns were silent, it was peaceful. But in the day . . . ' he closed his eyes and Elvina hardly dared to breathe.

Roderick swung round and looked at her. 'I can't tell you about it. It was too horrific to describe to a young girl who spent the war in the peace of this lovely place.'

'Perhaps it would help to talk about it,' she ventured at last.

'But not to you. I couldn't tell you about young men, still not much more than children, lying dead in the mud. Or about the wicked injuries they suffered from the enemy bullets.' He turned back to the sea. 'I had to draw these sights, pretend not to be affected by them. But the visions remain in my head and I can't get rid of them.' He gave a shuddering sigh.

Elvina took his arm and pulled him round. 'You must fill your mind with other sights. Look around you. The sea is beautiful. See how it creams its way over the sand. Look at the seabirds, gliding and swooping over the harbour.

'Look at the hills beyond the village covered with wild sea pinks and foxgloves. It's all so beautiful. Gaze at it every day and force the painful pictures out of your mind.'

She startled herself with her eloquence. But all her feelings for this lovely place came out forcefully as she tried to make him see what she saw and forget his terrors.

Roderick paused and turned towards her. 'What wisdom from such a young girl who's been nowhere and seen nothing.'

Hurt, Elvina's eyes flashed. 'Don't patronise me,' she stormed. 'I was only trying to help you.'

He caught her arm. 'I'm sorry,' he said quickly. 'That was unforgivable of me.' He sighed. 'You're right, of course. Polrame is beautiful and if anything can erase the nightmares, this place can.'

Elvina quickly brushed the tears from her eyes. 'I'll go home now,' she said, turning away. 'The aunts will wonder where I am.'

'No.' He caught her arm again. 'Don't go, please. Let's walk.'

Elvina looked up at him under the brim of her straw hat. Aunt Tilly was right. He'd had such dreadful experiences while she was safe at home in the little Cornish village. She nodded.

After dinner that night, Roderick remained behind in the dining-room after the other guests had left.

'Is there a picture house nearby?' he asked.

'Yes. In Penzance. But you might be too late now. I could ask the aunts to give you an early dinner if you want to go one night.'

'Do you like films?'

'Me? Oh yes. I go with Nancy sometimes. She's a real fan.'

'Would you come with me?'

'Well . . . ' She looked doubtful. 'I couldn't get away in the evening. Nancy and I usually go in the afternoon.'

'We could go in the afternoon. I've bought a car. It was delivered yesterday.'

Elvina looked at him, her eyes shining. 'I've never been to the pictures in a car.'

'So you'll come? Tomorrow afternoon?'

She hesitated for only a second, then gave him a wide smile. 'I'd love to.'

* ★ ★

I don't think it would be a good idea, my dear. I mean you don't know him well,' said Aunt Tilly.

'But . . . but . . . ' Elvina turned in despair from her to Aunt Susie. 'Why isn't it a good idea? It's only the pictures and it's in the afternoon.'

'Aunt Tilly's right,' said Aunt Susie.

'You hardly know the man. To go off gallivanting in a car alone with him and then to the pictures. Well!'

'But I go with Clay or Jack.'

'That's different. They're just friends and Nancy's brothers. You've always known them and besides, you always go on a bus.'

'You told me to be pleasant to Mr Landry.'

'Pleasant, yes, but not to go driving around in a car with him.'

Elvina folded her arms and looked sullenly out of the window. 'You didn't object when I went to the tennis courts with him.'

'Tennis is different,' said Aunt Tilly, with a sigh. 'It was daylight and in the open air. And you walked.'

There was silence in the kitchen for a few minutes. 'What have you got against cars?' asked Elvina.

'Oh, Elvina,' said Aunt Susie. 'If you can't see what we mean . . . ' She put her arm round the girl's waist and pulled her towards her. 'Don't let's fight. You're usually such a sensible girl. And don't forget, you said Jack was going to take you to the pictures.'

Elvina had forgotten. How could she go to see a film with Roderick today and then see the same one with Jack on Saturday? Her usual sunny temper re-asserted itself.

'Very well,' she said resignedly. 'I'll tell Mr Landry we're too busy for me to go.'

★ ★ ★

Saturday dawned dry and sunny. Elvina and Nancy, excused their usual family

64

duties, presented themselves bright and early at the church hall for the Sunday School Treat.

There was a buzz of activity. Eli Corey had delivered baskets of saffron buns, the air in the village was deliciously scented with saffron, and they were stacked up ready to be put on the charabanc when it arrived. Large containers of fresh lemonade for the children waited in other baskets.

The girls carried lists of the names of the children in their Sunday School groups. As soon as the children arrived, their names would be ticked off ready to board the bus. Elvina and Nancy hadn't long to wait. By nine o'clock, they were the centre of a crowd of excited little ones.

Each child was neatly dressed, however poor the family. The girls wore white dresses and black stockings. Elvina smiled at little Ellie Kent who peeped out from beneath the wide brim of a straw hat.

Her friend, Jennie, wore a hat like a

basin pulled down over her huge eyes. The two little girls held hands tightly. They were unused to going out for the day without their mothers.

The boys, in jerseys and trousers, all wore caps, many of which looked far too big for them, probably handed down from older brothers.

There was a cheer as two charabancs pulled up in front of the church hall. Ellie and Jennie jumped up and down in excitement.

Elvina and Nancy helped their pupils to climb aboard while the food was loaded at the back. When the two charabancs were full, and everyone was ready, they pulled away to loud shouts and cheers from the children.

After a mile or so, when everyone had settled down, someone started to sing.

'Miss,' said a small boy sitting behind Elvina, 'look at that corking car! It's following us.'

Elvina turned round in her seat. The green car was close to them, close enough to see the driver waving. Roderick! He was following them. As the charabancs turned off the main road, the car swung in behind them.

'What are you doing here?' asked Elvina as she climbed down from the bus.

'Your aunts told me where you'd gone. I thought I'd like to come on a Sunday School Treat. Do you mind?'

'Of course not. But I won't have a lot of time to talk to you. I have fifteen children to supervise.'

'I don't know anything about children,' said Roderick, 'but I'd like to help. What can I do?'

Elvina looked around. 'Jack,' she called to Nancy's brother, who was lifting baskets from the back of the charabanc. 'Can you do with some help?'

Her attention was taken by the children so she had no chance to see how Roderick was getting on with Jack.

She and Nancy formed their children

into a crocodile and marched them down to the huge bay spread out before them. Their own beach was a cove, encircled by cliff, which curved round on either side. This bay was wide and the outgoing tide revealed a huge stretch of sand, ideal for races and games.

It was decided to hold the children's races first before they became too tired. For two hours, Elvina was kept busy recording the result of each race. Roderick helped by marking starting and finishing lines with rows of pebbles. They had little time to talk, but to Elvina, he seemed to be enjoying himself.

Then it was time to eat. The baskets were unpacked and each child was given a saffron bun the size of a breakfast plate. Amazingly, most children managed to finish them.

At last, Roderick and Elvina could sit together and chat with cups of strong tea brewed over fires on the sand. But Elvina felt uncomfortable. Jack was sitting a few yards behind and she could feel his eyes boring into her.

When Roderick jumped up to assist with the loading of empty baskets into the bus, Jack came over to her.

'What's he doing here?' he demanded. 'Who is he, anyway?'

'He's staying at our hotel. His name is Roderick Landry.'

'Oh my,' said Jack, in an affected voice. 'Well what's he doing here? Did you invite him?'

'Don't be so aggressive,' said Elvina. 'No, I didn't invite him. He followed us. He wanted to see a Sunday School Treat. But I would have invited him if I'd known he wanted to come. Do you mind?'

'Yes I do,' Jack's voice was sulky. 'You should sit with us like you usually do, not with him.'

'Oh go away, Jack Perrans,' said Elvina, getting to her feet. 'You don't own me. I'll talk to whoever I like,' and she tramped off across the sand to round up her children.

In the afternoon, the grown-ups raced while the children watched. Elvina won the egg and spoon race and then the ladies' race, to wild applause. She went over to where Roderick was sitting and collapsed beside him.

'It's getting too hot for running,' she panted, 'I'm worn out.'

'You did very well,' he said, with a smile, handing her a bottle of lemonade. 'You're quite the athlete.'

Jack appeared in front of them. Grabbing Elvina's wrist, he pulled her to her feet.

'Come on, Elf, it's the three-legged race. We won last year. Let's see if we can do it again.'

With an apologetic smile at Roderick and a helpless shrug of the shoulders, she allowed herself to be led away. Jack tied their ankles together, they took their places in the line and at the signal, hobbled off across the bay.

They were first to finish, but as they

crossed the line, they tripped and fell in a heap on the golden sand. Elvina felt Jack's arms close round her firmly as they rolled over and over. Before she could extricate herself, he had kissed her on the lips.

'Let him dare to do that,' he muttered.

Elvina's face flushed bright red. She looked around, but no one seemed to have noticed. Jack had kissed her before, brotherly pecks on the cheek, but this was different. She untied their ankles, brushing his hand away furiously when he tried to help her.

She marched back to where Roderick had been sitting. He wasn't there. He must be helping, she thought. Then she looked towards the charabancs. The green car had been parked nearby. It was gone. She put her hands to her burning face. He'd been watching the race. He must have seen what happened at the finishing line.

Nancy came up to her. 'We're giving all the children a drink of lemonade,' she said, 'then we're leaving.' She looked at her friend curiously. 'Are you all right? You look very red in the face.'

'It's the sun. And running,' said Elvina, turning away. 'I'm fine.'

When the children were safely aboard the charabanc, Jack came over to Elvina. He looked sheepish.

'I'm sorry, Elf. I don't know what made me do that.'

She looked at him. He was staring down at his boots as if he couldn't face her. She gave a deep sigh. He was her friend; it wasn't worth falling out with him over one silly kiss.

She put a hand on his arm. 'I've already forgotten it, Jack. I'm not mad any more.'

'And you'll still come to the pictures with me tonight?'

Tonight! She'd forgotten that. There wouldn't be time to talk to Roderick. But she'd promised Jack. She nodded.

'Of course. What time?'

'We should leave as soon as we get back. Come and have a cup of tea at our house. It will save time and Mam always likes to see you.'

Elvina hesitated.

'Our Johnny can take a message to the Aunts,' he urged.

'Very well. Thank you, Jack.'

She climbed aboard the charabanc with mixed feelings. She was looking forward to a visit to the pictures, but if she didn't return to the hotel, Roderick would find out that she was with Jack.

'Didn't we have a lovely time, Miss?' said a small boy sitting next to her. 'I wish we could do it every week.'

Elvina smiled at his grubby little upturned face and patted his knee. 'You wouldn't enjoy it so much if we did, Albert,' she said. 'Why don't you have a little sleep like the others?'

Most of the children were quiet, their heads lolling forward in sleep. Sun, fresh air and exercise had worn them out.

Elvina put her head back and closed her eyes. She didn't want to sleep, just to think. Why had Roderick followed her? Was he really interested in joining the Sunday School Treat or did he want to spend the afternoon with her?

She couldn't desert her friends to spend time with him. She didn't know how long he would be staying in the village. She was beginning to find him intriguing and attractive. But was there any future in the relationship? If he went away, she'd be thrown back on her friendship with Clay and Jack, dependant on them for her outings.

She sighed deeply. Life was becoming complicated. What would Roderick say when she saw him again? What would she say? Oh bother the man, why had he ever come to the hotel?

Then her lips formed a little smile. But I'm glad he did, she said to herself. Life was becoming much more interesting with him than without him.

* * *

The Regal Palace was the most luxurious building Elvina had ever been in. The red carpet was thick; her feet sank into it. It felt like the softest sand.

Jack wanted to sit in the back row. Elvina knew what that meant and refused. She chose a row nearer the screen and settled herself comfortably in the cushioned seat.

She gazed around. The auditorium was beginning to fill up. She spotted Annie Kent looking for a seat, and waved.

'Nearly forgot,' said Jack, standing up. 'Promised you a box of chocolates, didn't I?'

'You did,' said Elvina, with a big smile. 'I hoped you'd remember.'

'Won't be long. Hope there isn't a queue.' He made his way out to the foyer and Elvina realised that Annie Kent had made her way along the row and was sitting in Jack's seat.

'My friend, Jill, is minding my seat,' she explained. 'I just had to speak to you. I wouldn't like you to hear it from anyone else and get the wrong idea.'

'What are you talking about?' asked Elvina.

'Your friend, Roderick,' Annie coloured slightly. 'Remember I met him at the tennis courts? Well, he brought me home from Truro in his car. It's a dream. I felt as if I was in a film myself.'

Elvina stared at her in amazement. 'Brought you home? When?'

'This afternoon. After he left the Sunday School Treat. He said he'd seen enough, so he left. He went to Truro. I was there on my own, shopping, and we bumped into each other.' She gave Elvina a curious look. 'Isn't that a funny thing to say, 'seen enough'. I wonder what he meant.

'I'm sure I don't know.' Elvina felt flustered. 'There's no reason why he shouldn't give anyone a lift. It's the sort of thing he would do. He's very kind.'

'There's something else.' Annie hesitated. 'Before we came home, we went to a teashop for a cup of tea.'

'It's nothing to do with me,' Elvina protested. 'Why shouldn't he take you for a cup of tea?' She wondered how much of this adventure Annie had told her mother.

Annie looked unhappy. 'I just wanted to tell you myself. After all, he's your friend.'

Before Elvina could answer, Jack appeared. With a quick greeting to him, Annie scuttled back to her friend.

'What did she want?' asked Jack.

'Nothing specially.' Elvina looked at the blue and gold box in his hand.

'For my lovely Elf,' said Jack, presenting the box to her.

I'm not his, thought Elvina, but she let it pass. It was a beautiful box of chocolates.

There was a cheer from the audience. Arms full of sheet music, the pianist, a small man with slicked down black hair, had appeared. Spotlights lit up the silken folds of the looped-up curtain. It began to roll up slowly to the crashing chords of the overture. The first film had begun.

It was an exciting tale of bank

robbers involving lots of racing in and out of buildings and on and off fast moving trains. Jack enjoyed it greatly, bouncing around in his seat and ducking down at the gunshots.

The next film was the story of a simple country girl whose father forced her to marry the wicked squire instead of her true love. Elvina sniffled her way through that one.

Then there was a comedy. The antics of a large dog and the tiny man who owned him had the whole picture house in hysterics.

'Wasn't that funny,' laughed Elvina wiping her eyes again, as the film came to an end.

At last the name of the main film and its star, Mila Bondi, appeared on the screen. Everyone settled back to enjoy it.

'Hope it's not going to be too soppy,' muttered Jack.

'Shush,' said Elvina, trying to open her crackly box of chocolates quietly.

The film was 'soppy,' but also very

exciting. There were car chases and a runaway horse and trap. The hero jumped from a high tree branch into a fast flowing river and the heroine was kidnapped by the villain. Of course it all ended happily with Mila Bondi wrapped in the arms of her handsome hero.

As their lips met, Elvina sighed deeply. She pulled her hands from Jack's. He had captured them during an exciting moment and refused to let go.

Jack looked at the clock on the wall next to the screen. 'If we hurry, we'll catch the half-past ten bus.' Holding Elvina's hand, he pulled her out through the crowds and into the warm summer evening.

The bus stop was near, the bus already waiting for the crowds turning out of the picture house. They climbed aboard.

'Did you enjoy that?' asked Jack.

'It was splendid, absolutely splendid. Thank you so much for taking me, Jack.' She held up the chocolate box.

'And I've got a whole layer left to share with the aunts.'

Greatly daring, Jack slid an arm round her shoulders and pulled her towards him. Elvina didn't protest.

'Let The Future Take Care Of Itself'

Elvina was unsure how to approach Roderick at breakfast next morning. She almost hoped he wouldn't appear. But he did and there was no smile for her.

His 'Good morning, Elvina,' was cool.

She stood expectantly at his table.

'Just porridge and toast, please,' he said, and picked up his newspaper dismissively.

Seething, Elvina went to the kitchen for his order. What had she done wrong? Merely entered a race with a friend.

She returned to the dining-room with a tray and silently placed a bowl of porridge in front of him.

When the meal ended, he hung back

as he often did. Elvina, who was stacking plates on a tray, gave him a quick glance from under her eyelashes but said nothing.

He walked towards the door then came back a few steps. 'Did you enjoy the film last night? Your aunts said you had gone with your boyfriend.'

She spun round. 'He's not my boyfriend. He's just a friend — a childhood friend, and Nancy's brother.'

'From what happened after the race, I thought he must be your boyfriend.'

Elvina straightened up. 'That was just a bit of nonsense on Jack's part. He apologised afterwards.' She glared at him, daring him to make another remark.

He looked straight at her. 'I thought we were friends. You seemed happy enough to spend time with me.'

'We are friends, that is, we hardly know each other, do we?' Elvina felt confused. How could she put her feelings into words? He failed to come to her rescue. She shrugged and turned back to her work.

'How long do you need to know someone to realise that there is a sympathy between you?'

'What do you mean, a sympathy?'

'I think you know what I mean.' He took a step towards her. 'We seemed in tune with each other. I should like us to become greater friends. Wouldn't you like that?'

'But you'll be gone soon,' she protested. 'We can be friends while you are here, but what of the future?'

'Let the future take care of itself,' he said. 'And I might not be gone soon.'

He left the room and Elvina heard him running up the stairs. Ten minutes later he came back down and then a car engine started up outside.

★ ★ ★

'I shall do the marketing this morning,' said Aunt Tilly. 'Would you like to visit Mrs Pensome? There's some soup you can take and warm up for her and some of those little cakes she enjoys.'

'Yes, I feel a bit guilty about Granny Pensome,' said Elvina. 'My mind has been on so many other things lately.' She gave her aunt a smile.

Mrs Pensome, or Granny Pensome, as the village children called her, was a very old lady who lived alone in the centre of the village. She was house-bound, but never lonely. Every day someone called in with food or a few flowers or just to have a gossip.

Elvina, in a new pink and white dress, made her way down the hill, carefully carrying a bowl with a cloth tied on top of it. At Granny's cottage, she pushed open the old front door with her shoulder. No one ever bothered to knock.

Granny was sitting in her armchair by the fire. She felt the cold and although it was summer, she had a fire every day.

'Elvina! Come in, my love. 'Tis good to see you.'

'I've brought some soup,' said Elvina.

'Would you like me to heat it up for you?'

'Bide a bit,' said the old lady. 'Let's look at you. You're that pretty in your summer dress. Sit down and talk for a bit. I've got a new paper.' She rummaged in a bag at her side and brought out a brightly coloured magazine. 'Do 'ee read it,' she said, settling back comfortably.

Elvina opened the magazine. It was Red Letter, Granny Pensome's favourite. She always produced one when Elvina visited. She began to read the first story aloud.

Granny's eyes closed. Elvina wondered whether she was asleep, but as she stopped reading, the old eyes shot open and a bony finger gestured for her to continue.

She finished the story and went into the little kitchen to make two cups of tea.

'Tell me what has been happening at your hotel,' said Granny, when they were settled again with their tea.

'We've got a nice new young man. His name is Roderick Landry.'

'What's 'ee come here for? Holiday?'

'I don't know,' Elvina admitted. 'He's been in the war. He needs a rest.'

'Landry,' said the old woman, thoughtfully. 'There used to be some people of that name in Polrame. Lived in a cottage down by the beach. Gone now, of course. Read me another tale. I do so love 'em.'

Elvina read another story then Granny looked at her pensively. 'I've got something to show 'ee.' Elvina laid aside the magazine. 'Go upstairs and bring me down the little box under my pillow,' instructed Granny Pensome.

Obediently, Elvina climbed the narrow wooden stairs and was soon back with the box. It was about the size of her hand and of carved wood.

'Open it,' said Granny.

Elvina pulled and tugged but the box wouldn't open. Granny chuckled and took it from her. 'Tis a secret catch. Watch.'

She pressed on the front, gave a quick twist and the lid shot up. Elvina gasped. 'That's clever. May I try?' After a few tries, she managed to raise the lid herself.

'Now look 'ee here,' said Granny. She took a piece of cloth from the box, opened it carefully and revealed the most exquisite brooch. Elvina's eyes opened wide. Granny handed her the jewel and Elvina touched it gently with one finger tip.

It was in the form of a golden flower. In the centre was a circle filled with tiny yellow stones which flashed in the firelight. The petals were of sapphires and there were two narrow emerald leaves on either side.

'It's beautiful,' breathed Elvina. She could hardly take her eyes from it.

'Many, many years ago, when I was a young thing like you, I had a sweetheart,' said Granny. 'Oh he was 'andsome. Black curls 'ee 'ad and sparkling white teeth. 'Ee was a sailor. Went all over the world. One day 'ee brought that brooch back for me from India or some such place. 'Ee said it was a promise for me. Next time 'ee came home, we'd be wed.'

'And were you?' asked Elvina.

Granny shook her head. 'Ee never came back. Ship went down with all hands. I never wed. 'Ee was my only love.'

'Oh, how sad.' Elvina's eyes filled with tears. 'But you had this lovely brooch to remind you of how much he loved you.'

Granny nodded, took the brooch, wrapped it in the cloth and replaced it in the box. 'Put it back, my lover,' she said, 'but don't 'ee mention it to any soul.'

'Of course not,' said Elvina. 'It's your secret.'

'Now it's our secret,' said Granny.

When she came back downstairs, the girl warmed the soup and placed it on a tray on Granny's lap. The next visitor would wash the bowl.

'I must go now, it will soon be time

to prepare lunch.'

Granny caught her hand. 'This man, what was his name?'

'Roderick Landry.'

'Aye. Do 'ee like 'im?'

Elvina coloured. 'Yes, yes I do like him.'

'And does 'ee like you?'

'I think so. Yes, I'm sure he does.'

'There's not many young men for you in the village,' the old woman said wisely. 'If you like each other, think carefully. 'Ee might be the one.'

'Oh Granny,' said Elvina with a laugh. 'I've only known him for a short time.'

'Time's not important,' said Granny Pensome. 'If you love each other, don't you let 'im go. If you wait, it might be too late.'

Impulsively, Elvina bent and kissed the wrinkled old cheek before she left the cottage.

★   ★   ★

One beautiful afternoon, Elvina decided to take a long walk along the coast road. She had hoped that Nancy would accompany her, but her friend was busy helping Eli to prepare cakes for a wedding next day.

The road was deserted. Elvina strolled along, enjoying the sunshine and the salty sea breezes, but wishing that she had a companion. She was a friendly girl and enjoyed company. She wished that Nancy wasn't so caught up in her friendship with Eli Corey.

Some way beyond the village, on the coast road that led past Elvina and Nancy's meeting place, stood Spindrift Cottage, probably the cottage Granny Pensome had mentioned. Its small garden touched the edge of the beach, so that the view was nothing but golden sand and wild sea waves.

The cottage was stone built and solid, but the blue painted wooden door was scarred by weather and lack of paint. One blue shutter hung down by a corner and the low fence around the garden was sagging and broken.

The cottage was too far from the village to be a playground for gangs of mischievous boys, and the local policeman, cycling to and fro from the next village, made it his business to keep an eye on it.

For as long as Elvina could remember Spindrift Cottage had stood lonely and neglected. She had never known it occupied. So this morning, she was amazed to see a man bent over, obviously tending the garden. Beyond him, two smaller figures also seemed to be gathering armfuls of greenery and throwing it onto a bonfire.

She quickened her pace. This would be an interesting piece of news for her aunts. As she drew nearer, the man stood up and turned towards her.

It can't be, she said to herself. Roderick? It was Roderick, but a Roderick dressed as she had never seen him before. He wore old sea boots, stained trousers and a worn jumper. On his head was a seawater-stained cap. He doffed the cap and gave her a sheepish grin.

'I didn't recognise you,' the girl said.

He looked down at his clothes. 'I bought them from an old chap in the village,' he explained. 'I didn't want to spoil my own clothes.'

'I expect he thought you were mad,' said Elvina with a laugh.

'Elf,' shouted a voice from the bonfire, 'we're helping Mr Landry. He's going to pay us.' It was Johnny, Nancy's youngest brother and his friend, Isaac.

'There's plenty for them to do while they're on holiday,' said Roderick. 'It helps me and it keeps them out of mischief. We're just going to stop for a drink. Would you like one?'

From a shady corner, he produced a large bottle of lemonade and a basket of cakes. 'Your aunts have been very generous. Come along, boys, time for a rest.'

The boys sprawled on the ground at her feet and Elvina reclined in state on Roderick's old coat.

'A picnic,' she said, delightedly. 'I love picnics.'

The boys soon finished off their cakes and lemonade and returned to the fire. Feeding a fire was obviously more fun than feeding themselves. Elvina and Roderick exchanged a smile.

'What are you doing here?' she asked curiously.

He looked back at the cottage. 'Doing up the ancestral home.'

'The ancestral home. Whatever do you mean? Whose house is it?'

'Mine.'

'Yours?' Elvina remembered Granny Pensome's words, '*There used to be some people of that name here. Lived in a cottage down by the beach.*'

'My grandfather built it many years ago. When I was a little lad, I came often for holidays with my parents. When I was about six, my father had a serious illness. We came here for a year so that he could breathe good sea air.'

'So you really do belong here,' said Elvina.

'My grandfather died last year. He left me the cottage. I decided to come down and see what was left of it. I intended to sell it. Now,' he gave Elvina a shy smile, 'I think I shall do it up and live in it.'

'But what will you do? Oh, of course, you're an artist. You can paint sea pictures and become famous.' Elvina began to feel quite excited at the idea.

Roderick stood up. 'I can't paint any more,' he said. 'I shall find something else to do. Perhaps I'll write.'

'But you're an artist,' she protested.

'No!' He spoke so loudly that the boys turned round and looked at them. Roderick lowered his voice. 'No, I can't paint. It's gone.'

Time to change the subject, she thought. 'Could I see inside?'

He opened the front door. 'You can see downstairs. I have to make sure the stairs are safe before I let anyone go up.'

Elvina looked around. 'Goodness, you've got some clearing up to do.'

Roderick laughed. 'The boys are keen

to help.' He kicked an old bird's nest with the toe of his boot. 'Looks like there's been some residents.'

Elvina wandered through to the kitchen. Rubble littered the floor. An old cooking stove rusted away against one wall and under the window, a sink was cracked and grimy.

'Lots of replacements needed in here,' said Roderick, following her in. 'But there's no hurry. I'm going to approach the re-birth of Spindrift Cottage as a summer project.

Elvina took a last look round. 'Time for me to go back. Thank you for the picnic. Can I come and help you some time?'

'I don't think your aunts would approve,' said Roderick. 'But you may come and see what progress we are making.'

Elvina called goodbye to the boys and began the long walk back to the hotel. So Roderick might stay in the village. Would that make any difference to their friendship, to his feelings for her?

★ ★ ★

There's to be a dance at the church hall tomorrow night,' Elvina told Roderick one evening. 'Would you like to come? Everyone will be there, even my aunts, though of course, they don't dance.'

'I don't dance,' he said, 'not any more. Thank you but I shall probably go for a walk.'

'You and your walks,' said Elvina. 'You can go for a walk every other night.'

'And I shall go for a walk that night,' he said, stiffly. 'I hope you enjoy yourself.'

I shall, thought Elvina defiantly, as she began to clear the tables. What is the matter with the man? Doesn't he like to have fun? Every time we seem to be comfortable together, he becomes prickly. Then she remembered his past and began to feel guilty.

'What's the matter?' asked Aunt Susie as she carried the dirty plates into the kitchen. 'You look miserable.'

'It's Mr Landry. I asked him to come to the dance and he said he'd rather go for a walk.'

'Perhaps he doesn't like dancing.'

'Perhaps. And perhaps he just doesn't like to enjoy himself. I'm sorry, Aunt, I'm trying to be friendly but every so often, he makes me feel as if I'm a silly little thing, just out to have fun.'

Aunt Susie patted her hand. 'Don't be so concerned about him. He's just adapting to ordinary life again. You go to the dance. You're young. That's the time to have fun.'

Elvina, in a cream dress with appliquéd flowers round the hem, went to the dance with Nancy, Jack, Clay, the oldest brother, Zed and his fiancée, Daisy.

'Quite a party,' said Nancy. 'We'll have to go early to get a table big enough for all of us.'

Music was playing as they got to the hall. 'Come on, Elf,' said Clay, 'have the first dance with me.'

'Fight you for it,' said Jack, dancing

about them with his fists raised.

'I'll have the next one with you,' promised Elvina.

Clay was quieter than Jack but equally devoted to Elvina. He worked at the garage in the village learning to be a mechanic. 'It's the coming thing,' he'd told Elvina some months ago. 'I'm saving hard. I've nearly got enough for a car of my own, a little two-seater. You'll be the first girl to have a ride in it.'

Now, as they circled the floor, Clay seemed to be bursting with excitement.

'So what's happened?' asked Elvina.

'What do you mean?'

'You look as if you're about to explode.'

Clay gave her a huge grin. 'You know the little car I told you about.'

'The one you're saving up for?'

He nodded vigorously. 'I'm getting it next week. I can't wait.'

'Oh Clay, how exciting. Don't forget I'm to be the first girl to have a ride. Don't take Annie Kent.' She'd said the words before she realised she was thinking them.

'Annie Kent! Why should I take Annie Kent?' Clay held her close. 'The first ride will be for my best girl. By the way, when did I last ask you to marry me?'

'That's blackmail,' said Elvina with a laugh. The music came to an end. 'Come on, back to the table. Jack will be waiting for his dance.'

In the interval, everyone queued up for the food. Elvina waited with Nancy.

'You didn't have a dance with your friend, Mr Landry,' Nancy observed.

'He didn't want to come. I invited him but he refused.'

'He was here half an hour ago.'

'Here? Where?' Elvina looked around.

'He stood at the back watching while you were dancing with Clay. I didn't see him after that. Perhaps he's gone.'

Elvina was silent, thinking. What was the matter with him? He watched her constantly, but when she invited him to accompany her, he refused. The man was a real enigma.

They had reached the front of the queue, were given a plate of food and returned to their table. Elvina looked into the crowd but there was no sign of Roderick.

At the table, Zed was teasing Daisy. 'I'll come up to the Hall and see this young lady,' he said. 'P'raps she'll take a fancy to me and take me back to London. I should like to be a kept man.' Daisy swung round to sit with her back to him.

'What are you two arguing about now?' asked Nancy.

'I was telling him about the young lady who's staying at the Hall,' said Daisy, 'and he said he wanted to see her. She might take a fancy to him and take him back to London.'

'You do think a lot of yourself,' said Nancy to her brother. 'Make yourself useful and go and get us some drinks.'

'Who is this young lady?' asked Elvina.

'She's called Miss Kitty Rawlings,'

said Daisy. 'She lives in London. She's Lady Crace's niece, though I don't think Lady Crace likes her very much.'

'These are scrumptious sandwiches.' Nancy waved her hand at Daisy. 'Go on, tell us the gossip. Why doesn't Lady Crace like her?'

'She's fast,' said Daisy solemnly. 'All painted up and her skirts are too short.'

'That's the fashion in London,' said Elvina. 'I've seen people like her in the fashion papers.'

Daisy's small mouth formed a prim little line. 'Well I don't like her, and neither does Lady Crace. Here's Zed with the drinks. Come on, Zed. Let's go and get our supper.'

The girls watched Zed and Daisy walk towards the supper table. Zed's arm was round Daisy's waist, all teasing forgotten.

Daisy was a housemaid at Penhallow Hall, the imposing Georgian mansion beyond the village. Her family lived in Penzance, too far to visit on her afternoons off, so she spent her time at

Nancy's cottage. Nancy's mother was very fond of her and though Nancy and Elvina laughed at Daisy's old-fashioned ways, they liked her too.

She was a small, plump girl, with soft curly brown hair. She was devoted to Lady Crace, the chatelaine at the Hall and her Ladyship seemed fond of the small, serious housemaid who was always at hand when she needed anything.

When they'd finished eating, Elvina had a surprise. 'Would you have the next dance with me, please?' asked a gentle voice behind her. It was Alfred, the young clergyman.

'I'd love to,' she replied, and as the music began again, they went onto the floor.

'Is your mother here?' Elvina couldn't imagine the severe Mrs Wilson at a village dance, not even to watch. But how had Alfred escaped her surveillance?

'She's spending the evening with friends we met at the church,' Alfred explained. 'I've come with their son.'

'And are you enjoying yourself?'

'I certainly am. I plan to dance every dance to make up for lost time.' Elvina joined in his delighted laugh and promised to introduce him to Nancy for the next dance.

Elvina noticed Nancy talking to Eli Corey. He had a hand on her arm but she pulled away. He walked off looking rather annoyed.

'Anything wrong?' asked Elvina, joining her friend.

'No.' Nancy pretended to be watching the dancing.

'Mr Bun — I'm sorry, I mean Mr Corey didn't look very pleased.'

'He wanted me to dance with him.'

'What's wrong with that? He's your employer.'

Nancy looked down at her shoes. 'I don't want people to see us together outside the bakery. You know how they talk.'

'You went out to dinner with him.'

'Yes, but that was quite a long way away. No one saw us.'

'Did you enjoy it?' asked Elvina, curiously.

Nancy flushed. 'I suppose you'd say I'd have enjoyed it more with someone my own age. But someone younger couldn't have afforded to take me to The Smugglers' Rest. The food was wonderful. I've never had a meal like that. And the car was splendid. I know you think I'm going out with him just because of his money . . . '

'No,' her friend protested.

'Well perhaps I am, but I've explained about that to you already.'

Elvina put her arm around Nancy's waist. 'I understand,' she said. 'Don't worry about it. Come on, let's go and find the boys. Clay proposed again this evening.' She laughed. 'The twins never give up.'

'I don't know why you are interested in Mr Landry,' said Nancy, as they made their way through the crowd. 'He's a grouch. My brothers are much more fun and they both love you.'

'So shall I marry them both?'

Before Nancy could reply, a burst of clapping from the stage silenced the assembled crowd. Mr Keane, the minister at the village church, stepped forward.

'Ladies and Gentlemen,' he began. 'The decision you've all been waiting for — the names of the people chosen to play the leading parts in the Festival of the Sea.' He held up a piece of paper.

'I think we have a few visitors here tonight, so for their sakes, I'll explain. Every year, our little village of Polrame holds a special festival, the Festival of the Sea. The origins are lost in time. We believe it has been held for three hundred years.

'The story goes that a long time ago, the harvest of fish from the sea was very poor for three consecutive years. The people were very worried. It was decided to hold a festival in honour of King Neptune and the Queen of the Sea. From then on, every year the catch has been good.'

Everyone clapped loudly and Mr

Keane held up his hand. 'This year, King Neptune will be played by Jack Perrans.' More applause. Jack was popular in the village. 'And the Queen of the Sea . . . ' he looked down at his paper, 'the Queen of the Sea will be Miss Elvina Simmons.'

Elvina gasped. From a little girl, when she was first a small mermaid then one of the Queen's attendants, she had always wanted to be the Queen. Jack rushed over, picked her up in his arms and spun her round. Everyone stamped and whistled.

Her aunts, who had joined the crowd as soon as their chores were finished, pushed their way through the cheering people and kissed their niece. Immediately, they began to discuss her costume which they would make.

After the excitement, there was time for just one more dance before the party broke up. Unable to choose between the twins, Elvina danced again with Alfred.

'I suppose it's a great honour to be

chosen to be the Queen,' he said.

Her smile was radiant. 'It's what every girl in the village dreams of,' she said. 'I feel so happy.

'You'll make a lovely queen with your fair hair and green eyes. Just like a mermaid,' he added shyly.

The evening ended. Alfred left her with a quiet word of thanks. She watched him cross the room. What a pity I'm not attracted to him, she thought. Life would be much more peaceful.

Elvina Is Unimpressed
By Kitty Rawlings

'There you are,' said Elvina as her friend made her way up the grassy bank to their meeting place. 'I thought you were never coming.'

Nancy flung herself down, panting. 'I had to finish the ironing,' she said. 'Mother's back is bad again.'

Elvina looked sympathetic, but she was too excited to talk about Nancy's problems.

'The Aunts have started to make my Queen of the Sea costume,' she burst out. 'It will be so beautiful. They've bought sea-green gauze and it will float over a pale green long pillar dress. They're as excited as I am.'

'You'll look lovely,' Nancy said loyally, but Elvina thought she detected a lack of real interest. Surely Nancy wasn't jealous? She knew her friend well enough to know that Nancy was a placid girl, never expecting very much. Jealousy wasn't part of her nature.

They sat in silence, looking out at the foam-flecked waves. Elvina didn't want to chatter on about her costume if Nancy had a problem. She waited for the other girl to speak, but Nancy just sat with her arms hugging her knees, looking out to sea.

'Out with it, Nan,' Elvina said at last. 'Is anything wrong?'

Nancy took a deep breath. 'Nothing's wrong, in fact, I should be very happy. That's how you're supposed to feel when you've had a proposal, isn't it?'

'A proposal!' Elvina stared at her friend with a delighted smile on her face. Then the smile faded. 'A proposal from . . . ' she prompted.

'Who do you think? Eli, of course.'

'Eli! Eli Cory! Oh Nancy, what did you say?' Elvina couldn't keep the horror out of her voice.

'I accepted him. I'm going to marry Eli Corey. I'm going to be the wife of the village baker.' Nancy's voice was toneless.

'But Nan, you can't.' Elvina's voice was quiet and urgent. 'Think about it a bit longer. Tell him you'll give him your answer next week.'

'I've given him my answer.' Nancy's voice was equally quiet, then to Elvina's distress, her friend burst into tears.

Elvina flung her arms round her. 'Don't cry, Nancy. Even if you've said yes, you can change your mind.'

Nancy sobbed for a few minutes then she sat up straight and groped in her pocket for a handkerchief. She blew her nose and wiped her eyes.

'I shan't change my mind,' she said. 'I told you before, I can't hope to make a better marriage. He's kind. He wants to look after me.'

'And he's well off. But money isn't everything, Nan.'

'I can help my family if I marry Eli. Mother doesn't think it's a dreadful idea. She thinks an older man will be right for me.'

She turned and looked at Elvina. 'I wasn't crying because of marrying Eli, I was crying because I knew you'd be beastly about it.'

Shocked, Elvina stared at her. 'But I'm only thinking of you,' she protested. 'You'd be happier with a young man your own age.'

'How do you know that?' Nancy flashed back, 'And where do I find this young man? There's no one here in the village. And if I do find him, he won't be likely to have any money. I'll have to scrimp and save like Mother. I don't want that sort of life.'

Again they sat in silence.

'You can despise me all you like,' said Nancy, 'I believe I'm doing the right thing.'

'I don't despise you,' said Elvina.

'It's all right for you. You've always had enough money. Your aunts aren't poor and one day the hotel will belong to you. What have I got to look forward to?' Nancy stood up. 'We've been friends forever. I wanted you to be pleased for me, but you're not. You're cruel and spiteful.'

Elvina looked at her, her eyes full of tears. Cruel and spiteful! Nancy had never used words like that to her before. They had never had an argument before. She felt her happy world breaking up around her.

'Nancy.' She scrambled to her feet and put out her arms. Nancy pushed her away.

'Leave me alone.' She stumbled down the bank and along the road towards the village. Elvina watched her go, unable to move, unable to follow.

★ ★ ★

She didn't know how long she had been sitting there lost in her misery, when she heard a voice from the road below. It was Roderick.

'What are you doing there. Are you coming down or shall I come up?'

She stood up. 'I'll come down.'

'Where's your friend?' he asked as she joined him.

'She's gone. She was here,' said Elvina in a quiet voice.

He gave her a thoughtful look. 'Anything wrong? Do you want to talk?'

She nodded without speaking and they began to walk slowly down the road towards Spindrift Cottage. Elvina told him about the argument.

'So Mr Corey has proposed,' he said. 'And you thought the idea of Nancy marrying him was ludicrous.'

'It is ludicrous. She's a young girl. He's an old man.'

They walked on in silence then he said, 'He's hardly an old man. Lots of young girls marry older men. In the past it was quite common. The girl got a comfortable life and someone to look after her; the man had a wife of whom he could be proud.'

Elvina said nothing and they walked on.

'Are you quite sure you don't object

because you don't want to lose your friend?' he asked gently.

'I shouldn't lose her. She'd still be in the village.'

'But married. Would Mr Corey mind her having a close friend? Some husbands do.'

'No, I'm sure he wouldn't mind. He's a nice man.'

'I'm glad you can say that. It shows you're being fair. So, Eli Corey is a nice man and materially, would be a good match for Nancy. Your only objection is their ages. Is that really enough?'

They'd reached Spindrift Cottage. Roderick had rebuilt a little wall between the garden and the road. They sat down there.

'She called me cruel and spiteful.' Tears filled Elvina's eyes again. 'She's never used words like that to me before.'

'She was upset and perhaps not quite sure she's done the right thing. Don't blame her. She'll come round. Give her time.'

Elvina sat and thought. Perhaps she was being horrid. Nancy was her best friend; she should be pleased if Nancy was happy. She'd go and see her, perhaps take her a present. She stood up.

'I'm glad we've talked. I feel better now.' She gestured towards the cottage. 'Have you done any more work here?'

'The boys have cleaned it out thoroughly. They are good little workers. Now I'm going to lay new floorboards and mend the shutters. I have a man coming next week to build a porch on the front.'

'I must get back to the hotel. You're staying here?'

'For a few hours. I'll see you at dinner.'

They parted and Elvina made her way back towards the village. On the outskirts, a large crowd had gathered and were standing in a circle, looking downwards.

'They're sinking a shaft for a well,' said someone as she joined the group.

'Look how deep it is.'

Elvina looked down into the dark hole, but it gave her a funny feeling in her stomach and she stepped back. She knew that wells were often sunk before a new cottage was built. It would be interesting to watch the progress of the new building.

When she reached home, Aunt Susie was sitting in the garden under an apple tree. She looked pleased when she saw her niece.

'Come and join me.'

'Shall I make us a cup of tea first?' asked Elvina. 'Actually I do want to talk to you.'

When they were settled, Small Aunt said, 'Guess who was sitting where you are and shelling peas for me an hour ago?'

'Reverend Alfred?' she suggested.

'Mr Landry,' said her aunt. 'He shelled a whole bowl full. He said he used to do it when he was a young boy. I think he enjoyed himself.'

'He's full of good deeds today,' said

Elvina. 'He's just been giving me advice about my row with Nancy.'

Aunt Susie looked at her in astonishment. 'Your what? Row with Nancy? I don't believe it. You and Nancy never row.'

'Well we did this morning. Aunt Susie, Nancy is going to be married.'

'That's wonderful. I'm so pleased for her. Who's the lucky boy? Do we know him?'

'You know him. He's not a boy. It's Eli Corey.'

Her aunt's jaw dropped, but only for a moment. 'That's a very good match for her,' she declared. 'She'll never want for anything with him. He's a good man. And he's been a widower for so long that there'll be no comparisons made.

'His wife had money, you know. He'll have quite a bit put away.' She picked up her cup and took a sip. 'Young Nancy and Eli Corey! Well, well, well!'

'Exactly.' Elvina couldn't keep a note of bitterness out of her voice. 'Young

Nancy and old Eli.'

'Was that why you quarrelled?' asked her aunt, sharply. 'Because you think he's too old for her.'

'Well he is. She's nineteen and he's forty-five.'

There was silence between them for a few minutes then her aunt gave a deep sigh. 'I knew a girl years ago, just like Nancy,' she said. 'She fell in love with a man much older than herself. Like Eli Corey, he had a successful business and a fine house. It would have been a good marriage for her.'

'Would have been. So she didn't marry him?'

'Her parents objected — very strongly. They said he was too old for her. She must wait for a young man.' She sighed again. 'She waited and waited. The man found someone else, but the girl never did.'

Elvina looked at her aunt. Her face, normally full of smiles, had sunk into lines of sadness. She had never married, was this her own story?'

'Not everyone is looking for passion-ate love,' said Aunt Susie. 'That doesn't last. Some girls just want their own home and someone to care for. Someone who will care for them. Age difference isn't important.'

Aunt Susie was speaking fervently now. 'If Nancy and Eli think they can be happy together, it is no concern of anyone else.'

Neither of them spoke and then in a different tone of voice her aunt said, 'Come along, carry these cups in for me please. We must start to get dinner.'

Elvina followed the older woman into the kitchen, thinking hard.

* * *

The dinner dishes had been washed and put away, the dining room tidied and Elvina was sitting in her bedroom wondering what to do about Nancy. They often spent the evenings together but now Elvina decided it might be best if they didn't see each other for a day or two.

She went to the window and leaned far out. To the left she could see the waves crashing onto the beach. A walk on the sands would be nice, but she couldn't risk running into Nancy.

The garden smelled fresh and cool in the evening air. She could take a book out onto the terrace for an hour. No one seemed to be there. She wondered where Roderick was — probably down at Spindrift Cottage.

She looked to the right and saw Clay coming round the side of the hotel. He glanced up, spotted her and waved vigorously.

'Come down. I've got something to show you.'

The car! It must be the car. She raced downstairs and out into the garden.

Clay took her hand and they went to the front of the hotel. There, in the road near the gate, stood the smartest little car Elvina had ever seen.

It was as dark green as a fir tree with a smart fabric hood folded down. The body had been buffed until it gleamed. She could imagine Clay working on it for hours with a cloth and polish.

'It's a Bullnose Morris Oxford,' he said, trying to sound casual. 'Nice little job, isn't it?'

'Oh Clay, it's beautiful. It must have taken you ages to save up enough money to buy it.'

'It's not new, of course,' he admitted. 'They stopped making them five years ago. And it needed quite a bit of work doing. But one of the other lads helped — he's been at the garage longer than me — and we soon got it up to scratch. Would you care for a spin?'

'Would I?' She gave him a dazzling smile. 'I can't wait.'

Clay took a heavy coat from the back of the car, shrugged it on and adjusted a pair of goggles.

'You do look funny,' she giggled.

'Run and get a warm coat,' he instructed, 'and a scarf to tie over your hat.'

'Do you mean it?'

'You'll be very cold if you don't, even on a warm evening like this. Go on, hurry up.'

Still giggling, she ran into the hotel and up to her bedroom. When she returned, Clay opened the single door and Elvina climbed in. She settled herself in the passenger seat and admired the interior of the car. He tucked a rug over her knees.

'What's this?' She pointed to a dial.

'It's a speedometer.'

'Whatever's that?'

'It tells us how fast we're going. Not many small cars have one,' he said with pride. 'It'll be jolly useful. Right. Are you ready?'

She nodded excitedly. 'Where are we going?'

'A mystery tour. Wait and see.'

He turned the car and they set off down the hill and out of the village.

'Not so fast,' Elvina gasped. 'It says twenty on your dial.'

'That's only twenty miles an hour.

She could do fifty if I opened her up.'

'Opened her up. Whatever do you mean? You are using some funny expressions tonight.'

'It's what we motorists say when we mean, go very fast.'

Elvina sat back and prepared to enjoy the unusual sensation of speed along the beach road. She was fascinated by Clay's skilful handling of the car and the pride and pleasure on his face.

'Slow down,' she shouted, 'there's Annie Kent. I want to wave to her.'

Clay obediently slowed down and as they passed Annie, who was walking with Jill Evans, the teacher at the village school, Elvina shouted, 'Annie, Annie,' and waved vigorously. She laughed out loud at Annie's expression.

'She's not the only one who goes driving in a car,' she said with satisfaction.

'Eh? What did you say?'

'Nothing,' she replied airily.

He swung off the road, turned left and passing two tall gateposts, set off

123

up a long drive. In front of them, in the gathering dusk, loomed a huge house.

'Wh . . . where are we?' asked Elvina in a worried tone.

'Penhallow Hall,' said Clay, sweeping round the side of the house and pulling up outside a row of stables.

'I don't think we should be here,' said Elvina. 'Oh, have we come to see Daisy?'

'In a moment. I want to speak to someone. Come on.' He held the little door for Elvina to climb out then led the way to an open stable door. But when she got near, Elvina could see that it wasn't a stable. Inside stood a large, gleaming white and silver car. A man was examining a wheel. He stood up as he noticed the young couple.

'Clay, what are you doing here?'

'Evening, Mr Rogers,' said Clay. 'Just brought my young lady,' he flashed a quick look at Elvina, 'for a spin. We thought we might be able to have a word with Daisy while we're here.

'Mr Rogers is chauffeur here,' he

explained to Elvina who looked puzzled. 'He gave me the driving coat. He had a spare . . .'

Mr Rogers slapped him on the back. 'It's good to see a young man determined to get on. He'll make a good mechanic when he's trained,' he said to the girl.

'What is a chauffeur?'

'I drive the cars for Lord Crace,' Mr Rogers explained, 'and look after them of course. Pleased to meet you Miss . . .'

'Simmons,' said Clay.

'Miss Simmons. Shall I take you to the servants' hall. Daisy will most likely be there.'

They followed him across the court-yard and into the side entrance of the house. It seemed full of gloomy corridors. They made their way down three before stopping at a heavy brown door.

Mr Rogers opened it and they found themselves in a long high-ceilinged room. Down the centre was a scrubbed table around which sat about thirty servants in varying uniforms. At the bottom of the table, amongst the housemaids, sat Daisy, Zed's betrothed.

The laughter and chatter died away as they entered. Then Daisy leapt from her seat and ran towards them.

'How did you get here? It's lovely to see you.'

'We came in Clay's new car,' explained Elvina proudly. 'Can you come out and see it?'

'You must have a cup of tea first,' said Daisy. 'I'll have a word with Cook.'

The large, motherly woman at the head of the table was already pouring out cups of tea and offering a plate of fruit cake. Daisy took Elvina to meet her friends and Clay was soon the centre of a group of young men, all eager to talk about cars.

★   ★   ★

Later on, back in the car and heading for home, Elvina threw back her head and laughed out loud.

'What a lovely evening,' she said, and all the better because it was unexpected. Didn't Daisy look happy. You can see she loves being there.'

Clay burst into noisy song, 'Daisy, Daisy, give me your answer do.' Elvina joined in and they sang happily all along the coast road.

'You shouldn't sing that,' she said, reproachfully. 'That's Zed's song. He's always singing it.'

'I shall make up a song for you,' he said. 'Elvina, Elvina, give me your answer do.' He gave her a wicked smile.

'We're here,' she said loudly, to drown the song, as the car pulled up outside the hotel. 'Thank you, Clay, that was a lovely spin.' She leaned across and kissed him on his cheek.

She moved back to her seat and looked out of the window to see Roderick waiting for her.

'Another childhood friend?' he asked caustically, an eyebrow raised.

'Yes,' said Elvina. 'This is Clay, Jack's

twin brother. Clay, Roderick Landry.'

'Clay has just taken me for a spin in his new car. It's a Bull . . . Bull . . . ' she looked at Clay.

'Bullnose Morris Oxford,' said Clay patting the bonnet as if it was a horse.

'I recognised it,' said Roderick. He walked round the little car. 'What can she do?'

'Fifty. She's got a speedometer.'

'Has she. And this is the gear stick on the outside?'

Elvina looked at the two men. What she'd thought would be a disagreement over her had turned into a discussion about cars. What was the matter with men these days? They seemed more interested in cars than girls.

★ ★ ★

Could you pop down to the village for me this morning?' Aunt Tilly asked when Elvina came down for breakfast. 'I don't know how it's happened, but we're right out of Sunlight soap.'

'Of course. I'll go straight after breakfast. Write a list for me.'

Elvina was pleased to go shopping. It meant she didn't have to help wash breakfast dishes. She crammed her hat on her head, picked up her basket and taking the list and the money, headed out of the door before Aunt Susie could decide that she'd go.

It was another lovely morning. The early sea mist had lifted; the air was fresh and tingling. Everything could be right with the world if only she and Nancy hadn't quarrelled.

As if the thought of Nancy had summoned her up, Elvina saw Eli Corey's bread delivery cart at the end of the village street. The horse was old and Eli let him go at his own pace. Elvina waited for it to pass before she crossed the road. As the cart drew near, she saw that Nancy was sitting with the baker.

Instinctively, Elvina raised her hand to wave. Nancy deliberately turned her head away. Elvina looked at her, stunned.

The cart disappeared and Elvina walked slowly on. Nancy was more offended than she had thought. What could she do?

She reached the grocer's shop and pushed open the door. The little bell above the door gave it's cheerful tinkle. She was the only customer so she had to forget Nancy and concentrate on her errand.

'Three bars of Sunlight soap and a tin of cocoa,' she read from her list.

Mr Penn placed them on the counter and looked at her expectantly.

'Two pounds of digestive biscuits and a half-pound bar of Cadbury's plain chocolate.'

'How are your aunts?' asked Mr Penn. He took biscuits from the large square tin, put them into a brown paper bag and weighed them. Then he placed them in her basket. They chatted for a few minutes then a customer arrived and Elvina left the shop.

Next door was the drapery shop of Mrs Enys. Aunt Susie had asked for two yards of black elastic.

I think that's everything, said Elvina to herself when she stood outside the shop. She consulted the list to check and as she looked up, she saw Roderick outside the church across the road. He was with a girl and they were talking and laughing as if they knew each other well.

Elvina knew at once that it was Kitty Rawlings, the girl whom Daisy had mentioned was staying at The Hall.

From across the road, Elvina could see that she had short bobbed shiny black hair and a very bright red lipstick. She was wearing a blue skirt just to her knees and a fetching little navy jacket with a bow at the throat.

Elvina decided she didn't want to meet her and walked on down the road, but Roderick's voice called her back.

'Elvina. One moment.'

She turned. He was coming across the road. He took her arm. 'I want you to meet the sister of a friend of mine.'

Elvina allowed herself to be escorted

across the road and the two girls were introduced. They eyed each other warily.

Roderick, sensing an atmosphere, smiled awkwardly. 'Kitty is staying at The Hall with Ralph,' he said. 'Ralph and I served together on the Somme.'

He turned to Kitty. 'Elvina is the niece of the ladies who run the hotel where I'm staying.'

Kitty looked at Elvina, languidly. 'You work there, I suppose.' She looked pointedly at Elvina's basket.

'I help, yes,' said Elvina. 'I don't like to be idle.'

Kitty gave a sigh. 'I don't suppose there's much to do in a place like this.' She looked around.

Elvina exchanged glances with Roderick. He was looking as if he wished he hadn't introduced the girls.

Kitty was studying Elvina's dress. 'Do you make your own clothes?' she asked.

'Sometimes,' said Elvina, with a defiant smile, 'or I go to the dressmaker. We have a very good dressmaker in the village.'

'Do you?' The other girl opened her eyes wide. 'I am surprised.'

I've had enough of Miss Kitty Rawlings, thought Elvina.

'It's nice to have met you,' she said untruthfully, 'but I must be getting back.'

Roderick looked relieved. 'I'll see you later,' he said.

Elvina walked home feeling depressed. First Nancy had turned away from her, then Roderick seemed to find Kitty Rawlings interesting company.

Nancy Continues To
Ignore Elvina

'I don't know how you managed to talk the aunts round, but I'm glad you did.' Elvina, in old clothes and a huge enveloping overall was sloshing white-wash onto the inside walls of Spindrift Cottage.

She was blissfully happy. Roderick hadn't mentioned Kitty Rawlings once and seemed as keen as ever to develop his friendship with Elvina. He had tackled the aunts one evening after dinner.

After complimenting them on the delicious meal, he had come straight to the point.

'I could do with some help and Elvina is very keen to contribute to the resurrection of Spindrift Cottage. It seems to fascinate her.'

The aunts had looked at each other and smiled. 'I think we both knew what fascinated you,' said Aunt Susie with a knowing smile.

Elvina had blushed but said nothing.

'He said he didn't want to take you away from helping us,' said Aunt Tilly, 'but perhaps you could go there in the afternoons.'

'Aunt Tilly and I talked about it,' said Small Aunt, 'and told him that you could treat it as a holiday and forget your work here for a few days. The hotel isn't full; we can manage.'

'He said he wouldn't work you too hard and would look after you.'

'I reminded him that we were trusting him with someone who was very precious to me, and Aunt Tilly said she hoped he would remember that he was an officer and a gentleman.'

'Oh Aunt,' Elvina looked embarrassed.

'Never mind, 'Oh Aunt', we need to get the situation quite straight. I take it you do want to help at the cottage.'

'Very much.' Her eyes were alight with enthusiasm. 'It was just a mess — broken walls and windows, rubbish everywhere and an overgrown garden. Now it's beginning to come back to life. Johnny and his friend have cleared away most of the mess. Now there's work to do to make it look as it did before — no, even better than it did before.'

It was her second day of whitewashing. Yesterday, she'd gone home with her hair covered with specks of whitewash and an aching arm. Today, she wore an old hat of Aunt Tilly's. It was shaped like a pudding basin. Roderick smiled every time he looked at her.

'You're a good worker,' he said approvingly. 'You've nearly finished that wall.'

He was busy with hammer and nails mending the old doors. The iron latches were still good; he'd decided to keep them. A wooden window frame and most of the cupboards in the kitchen needed replacing.

Roderick was good with his hands and Harry, the carpenter from the village, had promised to come for a day to do the jobs that Roderick couldn't manage. Harry was due to start the little front porch in a few days.

'There, that wall's done.' Elvina stood back and inspected her handiwork. 'I don't think I've missed anywhere.'

Roderick came and stood by her. 'A very good piece of work.' He put an arm round her shoulders and gave her a quick hug. For a second. Elvina enjoyed the closeness then she hastily stepped away from him.

'Perhaps we could stop for a cup of tea,' she suggested, to cover her embarrassment.

'The chimney has been cleaned and swept so it's safe to light a fire,' he said. 'We'll boil a kettle on that.'

Elvina fetched the covered basket Aunt Susie had given her. 'We'll have a bun with the tea,' she said. 'Hard work has made me feel quite hungry.'

While the kettle boiled, Roderick showed her what progress he had made with the window frame.

'What a wonderful view,' she sighed. 'I never tire of looking at it.' The sandy beach came up almost to the window. Waves broke on the small rocks at the edge of the water. The very end of the bay curved round into view on the left. 'I can see the sea from my bedroom window, but it's not as close as this.'

'I may decide not to live here,' said Roderick.

She turned her head quickly and looked at him. 'What do you mean?'

'I might sell it, or let it out for a holiday home. People are beginning to want seaside houses for holidays.'

'But where would you live?'

He was silent for a while, looking out of the window. At last he said, 'That's the problem, I don't know where to go or what to do.'

'Your parents?'

'Yes. I could go back to live with them, but it wouldn't be a good idea.

138

They have their own lives, and I've been away for several years. It probably wouldn't work out.'

Elvina almost mentioned his painting, then she remembered his reaction when she'd last done that, so she said nothing.

'That's why I came down here,' he said. 'I needed to get away to think. It's easier to think walking along cliff tops, with just the birds for company, than on the city streets.'

'That's why you go for walks in the evening.'

He nodded, and continued to stare out of the window.

She turned back to the fire. I don't want him to go, she thought. I want us to get to know each other better. He's sad and I know I can help him.

He turned from the window. 'I've a few ideas for the future. I'll tell you about them when I've sorted them out in my mind. Come along, back to work.' He took her hand and pulled her to her feet.

* ⋆ *

By four o'clock, Elvina had had enough of painting and decided to go home. Roderick wanted to stay for an hour or so.

'Johnny and his friend might be here soon,' he said.

Tired, Elvina walked slowly back to the village. As she passed the bakery, the door opened and Nancy came out. The two girls looked at each other.

'Hello, Nan,' said Elvina.

Nancy looked at her coldly. Elvina thought she wasn't going to speak, then she said, 'Good afternoon,' opened the door and went back inside.

Elvina stared at the closed door. She'd made the first move and been rebuffed. What more could she do? Eyes full of tears, she walked home.

Later, after dinner, she wandered down to the terrace with Roderick. They were both physically tired, and sat in companionable silence, looking out to sea.

At last he said, 'What are your plans for the future? Shall you always stay here in the hotel?'

She sighed. 'I'm like you. I don't know. Sometimes I hate the idea of always being here, never seeing anywhere else, but at other times, I can't imagine leaving.'

'You could start a new career as a decorator,' he said with a laugh.

She made a face at him. 'Perhaps I could train for something,' she said thoughtfully. 'A nurse or a shorthand typist in an office. Lots of girls are making careers for themselves now.'

'The war gave women chances they never had before,' he said. 'With the men away fighting, the women took over their jobs. They even worked in factories. Of course, when the men came home, they wanted their jobs back. But women will never settle for quiet domestic lives again.'

Elvina sat thinking. What did she want to do? Her life was changing slowly. Nancy would be married soon.

They could never return to the carefree friendship they'd had before if Nancy was a married woman.

She leaned back in her chair so that she could look at Roderick without his knowing. The paleness of his skin that had been so noticeable when he first arrived in Cornwall, was slowly changing to a light tan. All his walks by the sea had probably done that, she thought. He certainly had a healthy glow.

She studied the clean lines of his profile, his firm chin and neat ears. His dark hair was beginning to grow so that the severe soldier's haircut had almost vanished.

She sat up again. She was beginning to have feelings about him that disturbed her. Her friendship with Jack and Clay had been youthful and innocent. They were more like puppies with the same high spirits.

Roderick was different. He was quiet, thoughtful. He was a man while Clay and Jack still seemed boys. Roderick had experienced things that the boys could only imagine. That had formed his character and his emotions.

She had seen nothing of life herself. Could she cope with a man like Roderick?

What am I thinking? she asked herself. He doesn't want me. I'm just a little Cornish mouse to him, someone for a quiet friendship while he sorts out his future. It was not the time for silly daydreams.

'I think I'll have an early night,' she said. 'I'm quite tired.'

'So you should be. Do you really want to help tomorrow?'

'Oh yes. I'm going to finish that room. I'll see you in the morning.'

He stood up to wish her goodnight. Then he took her hand. 'Thank you, Elvina, you're a real friend.' Swiftly, he raised her fingers to his lips and kissed them.

She murmured a quiet goodnight and walked quickly back up the garden path. Inside her room, she pressed her fingers to her lips, finding the place where his had been.

She walked to the window and looked out at the darkened sea. In the distance, the lights of a ship shone like golden pinpricks as she moved slowly across the waves.

I feel like a ship, she thought, being tossed this way and that by the little events of my life.

* * *

On Sunday, Elvina went to church to conduct her Sunday School class. Usually she enjoyed the session. She taught small five-year-olds and found them very sweet and easy to control.

She and Nancy sat each end of a long room. Nancy had not yet arrived and Elvina wondered what sort of mood she would be in. The rebuff at the bakery shop had shaken her. She hadn't imagined that Nancy would keep up the bad feeling for days.

She arranged chairs in a small circle

and placed her chair so that she was sitting with her back to the other group.

In ones and twos the children arrived, laughing and chattering, but in a subdued manner. They felt the solemnity of being in the church building.

When Elvina stood up to give out some brightly coloured texts, she noticed that Nancy had come in and was sitting in her usual place with her group of slightly older children.

Elvina sat down again and began to tell the children the story of Joseph and his coat of many colours. When she had finished, each child took a piece of paper and sat on the floor with a box of crayons in the middle of the circle.

'Draw a picture of Joseph,' she instructed them, 'and make his coat as bright as you can.' She watched her group and commented on the drawings automatically, but her mind was on her friend at the end of the room.

At the end of the session, the children went home and Nancy and

Elvina tidied their ends of the room. Elvina picked up a box of crayons to return them to the cupboard at the exact moment when Nancy started to do the same thing. They met in the centre of the room.

'Nancy . . . ' Elvina began. Before she could say any more, her friend cut in. 'Good morning. That's all I intend to say to you. I'm speaking because we're in church and it would be un-Christian to ignore you.' She bent to replace her box of crayons in the cupboard.

'Nancy, please. Don't be silly.' Elvina's tone was agonised.

Nancy spun round. 'Don't you dare to call me silly. Your opinions might be unimportant, but you were my friend and you've really upset me.' She collected her coat and hat. 'I'm leaving now. My fiancé, Mr Corey, is waiting for me.'

Elvina watched her retreating figure. She could do no more. She'd made three attempts to speak to Nancy. It was plain their friendship was over. Her face was a mask of misery as she walked out of the church.

'What a miserable face,' said a voice, and two hands gripped her shoulders. She looked up into Roderick's face.

'I suppose it's Nancy?' he asked in a low voice.

She nodded. 'She just won't speak to me. I don't know what else I can do.'

'Come along.' He tucked her hand under his arm. 'Let's go for a walk on the sand.'

She looked doubtfully at her pale leather shoes.

'Perhaps not,' he said. 'You don't want to scratch those pretty shoes. We'll go down to the cottage. I'll show you what we did yesterday.'

She disengaged her arm from his. People seeing them walking arm in arm might get the wrong idea. He made no move to take her arm again.

She noticed what he wanted to show her before he could say a word. 'The porch! It's finished,' she said. 'I like it so much. And the little bench seats either side. How lovely to sit out here on a summer evening.

'I shall paint it pale blue tomorrow,' he said. Taking a key from his pocket, he fitted it into the lock and stood aside for her to enter.

'You have worked hard,' she said, looking around admiringly. A new wooden floor gleamed with varnish. The window frames had been cleaned and painted white and the heavy beams overhead were sooty black. 'You'll soon be able to move furniture in, then it will look like a real cottage.' Then her face fell.

'What's wrong?' he asked. 'Is there a problem?'

'I was just thinking that if it is finished soon and you decide to sell it, you'll go away.'

He came and stood next to her and took her hand. 'Perhaps not,' he said. 'Now shall I tell you where I went yesterday morning?'

'A walk, I expect.'

'No. A drive. Down to the village to Miller's Garage.'

'Was there something wrong with your car?'

'Not at all. I went to see Clay.'

'Clay?'

'We fixed up a visit the other evening when he took me for a spin.'

'But why would you want to visit a garage?' she asked.

'Cars are the coming thing, as I'm sure Clay told you. And where there are cars, you need garages.'

'I suppose that's right,' she agreed, 'but why did you . . . '

'I've had an idea at the back of my mind that I might like to own a garage. The more I drive my Calthorpe Minor, the more I feel I could get really interested in cars — all sorts of cars. I wanted to have a look around a garage, see what they did, what kind of equipment they had.'

'Is that what you might like to do in the future?' she asked, beginning to catch his enthusiasm.

He smiled at her. 'There are many problems to sort out first. Money, of course. My father will help and I have some money of my own, but I don't know really what is involved. The best thing would be to have a partner, I suppose. And then I'd have to decide where to have the garage.'

'So you might still go away. You wouldn't have it here, would you? No place would need two garages. There would never be enough cars to work on.'

He made no answer to this but gave her cheek a little pat. 'Cheer up,' he said. 'You're beginning to look gloomy again. It won't happen for some time — if at all.'

She smiled at him. 'It must be nearly lunchtime. Let's get back.'

★ ★ ★

She walked in to find two very solemn looking aunts.

'What's happened?' she asked. 'Have you burnt the lunch?' She removed her hat and smoothed her hair in front of the mirror.

'We've had some sad news this morning,' said Aunt Tilly.

Elvina spun round. 'Sad news?'

'Granny Pensome has died,' said Aunt Susie.

'Oh no!' Elvina looked stricken. 'But I saw her only a few days ago. She was fine. I read to her and we chatted . . . ' Her eyes filled with tears and she couldn't go on.

'A neighbour popped in to see her after breakfast this morning,' said Aunt Tilly, quietly. 'She was sitting in her armchair by the fire as usual, but she was dead.'

Elvina sat down in a chair by the table. 'Poor Granny,' she said, and the tears began to flow.

'The doctor said that it would have been very quick and that she didn't suffer,' said Aunt Tilly. 'We must be thankful for that.'

Elvina nodded. She felt very sorry; she had been really fond of old Granny Pensome.

'Who will arrange everything?' she

asked, 'you know, the funeral and so on.'

'Apparently there's a nephew,' said Aunt Susie. 'He lives up in London, I think, and he's quite well off. They've sent for him.'

'I wonder why we never saw him,' mused Elvina. 'We always thought she was quite alone in the world.'

'I think there was a family row,' said Small Aunt. 'That often happens.'

★ ★ ★

The next day, a large man with a black toothbrush moustache turned up at the hotel and asked for a room for a few days. He signed the register, Gerald Pensome.

'You are Granny Pensome's nephew?' asked Aunt Susie.

'Yes. You knew her? But of course you must have done in a small village like this. Sad business. But she had a good life. She was eighty-eight, you know.'

She might have had a happier life if

you'd visited her, thought Elvina who was crossing the entrance hall at that moment. Poor Granny, dependant on friends and neighbours, but with no one of her own.

'Elvina,' called her aunt. 'Show Mr Pensome to room seven, will you, dear?'

Elvina wanted to dislike Gerald Pensome, but it was difficult. He was friendly, admired the room and asked questions about the village.

'How long are you staying?' she asked.

'I have to get back to London as soon as possible,' he replied, 'but there's the funeral and the reading of the will, so I'll be here for about a week, I expect.'

Elvina felt it might be inappropriate to say, 'Enjoy your stay,' so she just nodded and gave him a little smile.

It rained that afternoon, a sudden squall that blew shafts of rain against the window and kept everyone indoors. Elvina stayed in her bedroom. She decided to work on a cushion she had been given for Christmas and hadn't yet tried. It was pretty; a riverside scene with a family in the foreground sitting in the grass, enjoying a picnic. But Elvina couldn't get started. She was thinking first of Nancy, then of Granny Pensome.

At last she pushed the needlework away. I wonder where Roderick is, she thought. He's probably at Spindrift Cottage. She could hardly go there in the rain. Besides, her aunts wouldn't approve of that sort of outing on a Sunday afternoon.

She flung herself on her bed and lay with her hands behind her head. What would Roderick decide to do about his garage idea? What if he went back to where he'd come from and opened a garage there? Well there was nothing she could do about it. But she'd miss him dreadfully.

She sat up and swung her legs over the side of the bed. Why would I miss him? In the beginning, I disliked him. Then we became friends. Now — now I think I love him.

She stood up and looked at her reflection in the mirror. 'I think I love him,' she repeated out loud.

She sat down again on the bed. 'Roderick Landry, I love you,' she whispered, 'but could you ever love me?'

In the evening, the rain stopped and a sort of hazy sunshine appeared. Elvina made a sudden decision.

In her bedroom she took the red velvet cape from the wardrobe, lay it on the bed and folded it carefully. Then she slid it into a large bag, put on her hat and left the hotel.

She walked down the hill, and along the lane to Nancy's cottage. Before she could change her mind, she knocked on the door.

'We're Supposed To Be Just Friends'

Nancy's young brother, Johnny, opened the door. He broke into a wide smile when he saw Elvina.

'Hello, we haven't seen you for a while.'

'Who is it, Johnny?' a voice called from within.

'It's Elf, Mam,' said Johnny. He opened the door wider. 'Come in.'

Elvina hesitated. 'Is Nancy in?'

'She'll be back at any minute. She's helping Mr Corey with a special order.' He pulled Elvina inside and closed the door. 'Mam'll be glad to see you. She's fed up with me.'

Elvina followed him into the kitchen at the back of the house. Mrs Perrans rested on a day bed near the window. Her face was lined with years of pain, but her blue eyes still shone as brightly as when she was young. A bad fall on the farm where she worked as a girl had left her with a weak back which childbirth had aggravated. She spent much of her time on the day bed directing her children in the jobs about the house. As the only girl, Nancy came in for most of this.

'Elvina!' Mrs Perrans's face lit up when she saw the girl. 'Come in and talk to me, do. That young one only wants to talk about food or football.'

Johnny grinned. 'Can I go now, Mam? You've got Elf to talk to.'

His mother shook her head. 'See what I mean? He's no company at all.' She looked at Johnny who was hovering in the doorway. 'Off you go then, but remember, it's Sunday. Behave yourself.'

Johnny went quickly before she could change her mind.

'Sit down, my dear. Now what's all this about you and Nan having a quarrel? She's very upset, you know.'

'Of course, and so am I?' said Elvina. 'We've never had as much as a cross word. I only want her to be happy.'

Mrs Perrans patted her hand. 'It's what we both want,' she said. 'But maybe we see things differently. You're young. You think romance is the most important thing. Nancy's different — more down to earth. She wants a comfortable life, someone to take care of her.'

'But he's so much older,' Elvina protested.

'That's not really important. Nancy has thought about it. Most likely she'll be a widow quite young. She's prepared for that. And she'll be comfortably off. Don't you worry about Nancy.'

As she finished speaking, the door opened and Nancy came in. She stopped when she saw Elvina. 'What are you . . . '

'Nancy. I had to see you. I can't bear this ill-feeling,' Elvina said beseechingly.

'This argument has gone on long enough,' said Nancy's mother firmly.

'Now make some tea, Nan, and we'll all have a cup. Nothing like a cup of tea to sort out problems.'

Nancy made the tea and filled a plate with raspberry buns. 'These are what I've been doing this afternoon,' she said.

Elvina picked up the bag which she'd placed by her chair. 'I've brought you a present,' she said shyly, handing the bag to her friend.

'I don't need a present to . . . ' Nancy began, but a warning look from her mother stopped her. She opened the bag and drew out the red velvet cape. She looked from the cape to Elvina and back again.

'But this is your best cape. You can't just give it away.'

'I can. You'll get more use out of it than me. I'm sure your fiancé will take you to lots of places where you can wear it.'

'Oh, Elvina!' Nancy threw herself to the floor beside her friend's chair and they hugged each other. 'I've missed you.' This time, the tears on Elvina's cheeks were tears of joy.

When they were settled with fresh cups of tea, they began to talk about the wedding.

'We don't want a long engagement,' said Nancy, 'so we thought we'd have the wedding at the beginning of September. You and Daisy will be bridesmaids and we'll have the reception at the Smugglers' Rest.'

Elvina looked at her. She was listening to a very grown-up Nancy. She'd assumed that Elvina would be her bridesmaid so no more discussion was needed.

They talked a little longer about dresses and flowers and food, then Elvina stood up. 'I must be getting back. The Aunts will wonder where I am.'

Nancy accompanied her to the door. 'Come down this evening,' she said, 'and we'll talk a bit more. We'll take Skipper for a run.' She flung her arms around Elvina. 'I'm so happy we're friends again.'

Elvina returned the embrace. 'So am I. I'll see you this evening.' She started to walk away when she noticed a dejected-looking small figure turn into the end of the lane. It was a young girl. She walked wearily with her head lowered. In her hand was a large carpet bag.

'It's Daisy,' said Nancy, beginning to run towards the girl. Elvina watched as Nancy took the bag from Daisy and with an arm around her shoulders, took the girl into the cottage. Daisy was weeping gently as if she'd been crying for a long time. Elvina followed them back into the house.

Nancy put Daisy into a chair next to Mrs Perrans. The older woman held Daisy close to her until the girl had stopped crying enough to tell them what was wrong.

'I've been dismissed,' she said. 'Sent away without a reference.'

They looked at her in horror. To be dismissed without a reference made it almost impossible to get another position.

'Why,' asked Nancy. 'What did you do?'

'Nothing,' Daisy protested. 'It's all a lie, but they believed her not me.'

'Who? Tell us from the beginning,' said Mrs Perrans.

Daisy gave a shuddering sigh. 'It was that Miss Kitty Rawlings,' she said. 'She's not a nice girl. Expects to be waited on hand and foot. Never does a thing for herself and doesn't care what she says.'

'And did she say something bad about you?' queried Nancy.

'Said I stole her ring. I never touched it. I took her her morning tea and tidied her room a bit — picked up clothes she'd dropped on the floor and so on, but I never went near the dressing-table where she said she'd left it.'

'What did Lady Crace say?' asked Elvina. 'She's fond of you, isn't she? She wouldn't believe you'd steal anything.'

Daisy was a poor girl from a very rough part of Penzance, but she was gentle and scrupulously honest. No one who knew her would believe she could steal.

'She said she believed me at first,' said Daisy, 'but when they'd searched everywhere and questioned everyone, they began to believe Miss Rawlings. And she was making such a fuss. Said the ring was very valuable and insisted that I was dismissed on the spot. They kept back my box to search my things. Said they'd send it on.' Daisy began to cry again.

'What's going on?' came a man's voice from the doorway. Daisy leapt from her seat, flew across the room and flung herself into Zed's arms. 'There, there, my girl. Don't take on.' Zed patted her back and held her close. 'What's happened?' he asked his mother.

Daisy was crying again so Nancy and Mrs Perrans told him. He sat down and took Daisy on his lap. 'Don't you cry, sweetheart,' he said. 'Wicked liars they are. I wouldn't let you go back if they begged you.'

'But I won't get another position without a reference,' Daisy protested. 'What shall I do?'

'There's a position for you here,' said Zed. 'We'll be married sooner than we planned and you'll come and live here and help Mam. Nancy will be off to her fine house,' he made a face at his sister, 'and you'll take her place here.'

Daisy looked at Mrs Perrans who smiled at her and nodded. Then she flung her arms around Zed's neck.

'Oh Zed, I do love you,' she said.

'I should hope so,' replied her fiancé, 'especially as I've got some good news for you. I've been promoted. From Monday I'll be under foreman, with a good rise in pay.'

Zed had worked at the local tin mine since he left school. He was a serious young man with his brothers' features but none of their playfulness. He was well thought of in the village and had taken his father's place in the family after a rock fall in the mine had claimed the life of Mr Perrans, ten years before.

'It's no more than you deserve,' said his mother. 'You're a good worker and at last they've recognised it.'

Elvina added her congratulations. 'So now we'll have two weddings,' she said.

'Ours will be a proper village wedding,' said Daisy. 'We haven't got the money for a grand one like Nancy's.'

'And none the worse for that,' said Zed. 'As long as we're properly wed. I don't care about the frills and fancies. We'll go into Penzance and get you a pretty dress, and with some flowers in your hair, you'll be the prettiest bride in Cornwall.'

Elvina gazed at the little maidservant. Her funny little kitten face was bright with pleasure. She gazed at Zed in adoration. He thought she was beautiful, so she was. The power of love, thought Elvina enviously.

Realising how late it had become, she made her goodbyes and hurried home. She had a lot to tell the Aunts while they prepared dinner.

* * *

'Aunts,' said Elvina next morning at breakfast. 'I've been doing some thinking.'

'Oh yes.' Aunt Tilly poured her a cup of tea. 'Shall we like it?'

'I'm not sure, but I think it would be a good idea.'

'Well tell us about it,' said Aunt Susie, 'then we can decide.'

'It's Daisy. You remember I told you yesterday that she had lost her position?'

'Yes, poor girl.' Small Aunt was sympathetic. 'She's living at the Perran's cottage, you said. It must be very crowded.'

'Exactly,' Elvina agreed eagerly. 'So I wondered whether she could come here.'

'Here?' Tall Aunt looked at her suspiciously. 'In what capacity?'

'As a maid. She's trained, and you were saying the other day that we really ought to replace Agnes. She could

166

have Agnes's room. She's very quiet and pleasant. The guests would like her.'

Aunt Tilly looked thoughtful. 'What about the accusation of theft?'

'That was nonsense,' Elvina flared. 'Just that dreadful Kitty Rawlings being spiteful.'

'Mmm. Miss Rawlings is a friend of Mr Landry, isn't she? Are you sure that doesn't colour your judgment?'

Elvina flushed. 'That has nothing to do with it. Daisy is engaged to Zed Perrans. All the family know her well. Mrs Perrans will vouch for her. Go and see her.'

'That won't be necessary,' said Aunt Susie. 'If you and Nancy feel she can be trusted and was falsely accused, that will be good enough for us.' She looked at her sister, who nodded.

'We did intend to replace Agnes,' agreed Aunt Tilly, 'so we might as well try Daisy. Go and speak to her this afternoon, Elvina, and bring her to see us.'

★ ★ ★

On the following Thursday, Elvina, dressed in sober grey, accompanied her two black-clad aunts to Granny Pensome's funeral. All the village was there.

On foot, they followed the hearse drawn by plumed horses to the churchyard. Unusually, there was a cold wind and Elvina shivered, partly from cold and partly from sadness.

She was glad when the service was over and they could go back to Granny Pensome's cottage. Friends and neighbours had provided enough food for a feast. The aunts had brought two large veal and ham pies. Elvina tried, but could eat nothing. She just wanted to return to the hotel.

Mr Pensome, Granny's nephew walked with them. 'It was kind of you to come,' he said.

'It was the proper thing to do,' Aunt Tilly replied. 'She was a neighbour and a friend.'

Elvina said nothing. She couldn't

wait to get out of her colourless clothes and into a more cheerful dress.

Mr Pensome stayed at the hotel for more than a week. On the last night, at dinner, he asked if he could speak to Elvina when the meal was finished.

They went into the lounge, which was empty except for an elderly couple dozing near the fire. Aunt Tilly sat next to Elvina.

'My aunt was very fond of Miss Elvina,' Mr Pensome began. 'She left a letter for me saying so. She also said she wanted you to have this.' He handed the girl a small wooden box.

'I know what this is,' she said excitedly. 'Granny showed it to me one day. But I couldn't possibly have it. It looks valuable.'

Mr Pensome smiled reassuringly. 'She wanted you to have it,' he said.

'Open the box, Elvina,' said Aunt Tilly. 'Let's see what Mrs Pensome has left you.'

Elvina just sat with the box in her hand, looking at it.

'Oh let me open it,' said her aunt, impatiently, taking the little box from her niece. She pulled and pressed but the box remained closed.

'You're having no more success than I,' said the man. 'It must be a trick box. I'm sure Miss Elvina was shown how it works.'

Elvina took the box, pressed and twisted as Granny had shown her, and the lid opened. She took the piece of cloth from inside and unfolding it, revealed the brooch.

Mr Pensome leaned forward to get a better view. Aunt Tilly looked at it in silence. Then she shook her head.

'I agree. It looks valuable,' she said. 'My niece cannot possibly accept it.'

'It may be valuable,' agreed Mr Pensome, 'but whether it is or not, it now belongs to Miss Elvina. It was what my aunt wanted.' He stood up. 'I shall leave first thing after breakfast. Thank you for an excellent dinner.' He gave them a slight bow and was gone.

Elvina and Aunt Tilly sat looking at

the brooch. 'I think we should get it valued,' said Aunt Tilly. 'Until then I'll put it in the safe.' She took the little box and left the room.

Elvina remained sitting in her armchair, looking into the fire and thinking of Granny Pensome. How kind of her to leave the brooch to me, she thought. It doesn't matter whether or not it's valuable, I shall treasure it because of Granny and the story of the young sailor she loved so much.

★ ★ ★

The following afternoon, Elvina and Nancy were once again in their special place on the little hill opposite the beach.

'It's so peaceful,' murmured Elvina. 'Not a human sound.'

'It's so quiet, I could fall asleep,' agreed Nancy.

Suddenly, the peace was rent by a loud shout, 'Help! Help!'

The girls sat up as one. 'It's Isaac,

Johnny's friend,' said Nancy, standing up for a better view of the boy who was running up the road towards the village.

'Isaac! Hi!' Nancy waved her arms. 'Up here. What's wrong?'

'It's Johnny.' Isaac barely paused in his flight. 'He's stuck on the cliff. I must get help.' He raced on.

Nancy and Elvina scrambled down to the road. 'He must be this way,' gasped Nancy. 'Isaac came from there.'

The two girls ran down the road in the direction of Spindrift Cottage.

'I wonder whether Roderick is there. He could help,' said Elvina.

They reached the cottage. The door was open. They ran in, calling for Roderick, but it was obvious there was no one at home.

'Come on,' said Nancy, 'let's go further down the road and see if we can find Johnny. We can at least keep him company until the men arrive. He must be terrified.'

'Let's call,' suggested Elvina. They

began to shout Johnny's name as they ran.

'Listen, what's that?' Nancy stopped. They both listened intently. The tide was coming in but over the crashing of the waves they heard a voice.

'It's Johnny.'

The voice came from somewhere below them on the cliff face. Falling onto their stomachs, they edged forward and looked over the cliff. About fifteen feet below they could see Johnny clinging to a tree which stuck out precariously from the rock face. He was balanced on a shelf and the face he turned up to them was white and scared.

But he was not alone. A man stood close beside, holding the boy with one hand and a rocky outcrop with the other.

'Roderick,' called Elvina. 'How did you get down there? Do take care.'

Roderick didn't answer. He might not have heard. He was intent on making sure the boy didn't fall.

'Isaac must have reached the village

173

by now.' Nancy sounded frantic. 'Where are the men!'

Elvina stood up and walked into the road to see better. 'They're coming,' she shouted. A crowd of small figures could be seen in the distance.

'Hang on,' shouted Nancy, 'the men are coming.'

Feet clattering on the road came nearer and nearer and soon a group of village men with ropes and ladders were peering over the cliff and shouting instructions to each other.

One wiry man, nimble as a monkey, was lowered over the cliff on a rope and climbed down until he could stand beside Johnny. He carried another rope which he tied around the boy. At a signal, that rope was pulled up until Johnny was at the top in the safety of his sister's arms.

Another rope was lowered. Roderick tied it round his waist and soon he too was safely at the top. When their rescuer had joined them, everyone cheered.

'How did you get down?' Roderick

was asked. 'It's a dangerous climb.'

Roderick looked over the cliff. 'It is, isn't it?' he agreed. 'I heard the boy shouting when I was working in the garden so I climbed down. I must confess I don't know how.'

Several men clapped him on the back. 'It was a brave thing to do,' said one.

'Boy could have fallen without you to hold him,' said another.

'What were you doing on the cliff?' Nancy asked her brother.

He hung his head.

'Birds' eggs, I suppose,' said Nancy. 'You know what Zed said about taking risks.'

Elvina looked at Roderick with shining eyes. 'You've saved Johnny's life,' she said.

Roderick brushed aside the praise. 'He was safe as long as he hung on and didn't look down.'

'But he was frightened. He might have let go and then . . . ' Nancy couldn't finish.

Johnny came across to Roderick and flung his arms around the man's waist. 'Thank you, Mr Landry,' he said, emotionally. 'I'll help you all next week for nothing.'

The girls laughed and Roderick joined in. 'I'll hold you to that,' he said.

The screech of brakes as a low-slung, expensive looking motor car came to a halt beside them, startled them all. They turned to see Kitty Rawlings in a cream car coat with a big fur collar, opening the door and stepping out.

'What's all the excitement?' she asked. 'I've just passed a crowd of yokels laughing and shouting and heading towards the village.'

'They've just pulled this young man up from the cliff face.' Roderick ruffled Johnny's hair as he passed him.

'Mr Landry climbed down and stayed with me until they came,' said the boy.

Kitty Rawlings eyed Roderick up and down. 'Well, well, well. A hero, I declare,' she drawled. 'I just came over to see what you're doing now with your bijou residence.'

Elvina tapped Roderick on the arm. He seemed to have forgotten that she and Nancy were there.

'We're going now. I'll see you later.'

'I'm so sorry,' he said. 'Kitty, you remember Elvina, don't you? You met in the village. And this is her friend, Miss Nancy Perrans, Johnny's sister.'

Kitty gave them a cold little nod of her head. Elvina took Nancy's arm and they began to walk away. As they went, she heard Kitty say, 'I'm sorry, I didn't realise you'd be entertaining your little waitress friend.'

She didn't hear Roderick's reply. He escorted his visitor into the cottage and the door closed.

'So that's Miss Kitty Rawlings, is it?' Nancy sounded very annoyed. She's the one who accused poor Daisy. Your Roderick is welcome to her.'

'He's not my Roderick,' said Elvina, automatically, but her mind was on the two in the cottage. How long would

Kitty stay? Did Roderick welcome her dropping in? She was quiet as they walked back.

'Could you persuade him to come and see Mother this evening?' asked Nancy. 'I know she'd like to thank him for what he did.'

'I don't know,' said Elvina. 'I'll ask him, but he seems shy of mixing with people. And he won't want to be thanked.' They walked on for a while, then she said, bitterly, 'Anyway, he may spend the evening with Kitty Rawlings.'

'How does he know her?'

'Her brother served with him in the war. They were friends.'

'Where do they live?'

'In London. They share a house. I wish she'd go back there,' Elvina said fervently.

Nancy put an arm round her friend's waist. 'Don't worry about her. She's only on a visit. She'll go back soon.'

'Perhaps she'll take Roderick with her,' said Elvina, gloomily.

'You're sweet on him, aren't you?'

'No, of course not.' Elvina felt the colour rise in her cheeks. Nancy stared at her without speaking. 'Well — well, I suppose I am,' Elvina admitted. 'But don't say a word to anyone. I should die if he found out. We're supposed to be just friends.'

Elvina was laying the tables for dinner when she heard Roderick's car pull up outside. She thought — hoped — he'd come to find her, but he went straight upstairs.

After gardening and climbing cliffs, he'll want a bath and a change of clothes before anyone sees him, she told herself. I'll see him at dinner.

But he still hadn't appeared by the time she'd finished serving soup.

'Mr Landry hasn't come down,' she reported to Aunt Susie in the kitchen.

'No. He's gone out to dinner. Didn't he tell you?'

'Why should he tell me?' the girl asked, pertly.

Small Aunt gave her a sharp look. 'You've been spending quite a lot of time with him lately. I thought you two were becoming rather friendly.'

'He spent the afternoon with Kitty Rawlings who's staying at the hall. I expect he's taken her out to dinner.'

'To be honest, he probably has more in common with her than with you,' observed her aunt. 'I don't want to be cruel, but you must face facts or you may be hurt.'

'I heard her refer to me as 'his little waitress friend',' Elvina said bitterly.

'What did he say?'

'I don't know. They went into the house and closed the door.'

Aunt Susie placed dishes of vegetables on a tray and handed it to Elvina.

'He's just a friend,' she said. 'Remember that and keep it that way. It's safest.'

Roderick's Pain Is Still On Show

Nancy's wedding day dawned grey and damp. A fine sea mist mixed with a soft drizzle — mizzle, the Cornish called it, blotted out the landscape.

Looking from her bedroom window, Elvina felt bitterly that the weather was appropriate. Outwardly, she appeared happy about her friend's wedding; inwardly, she was as disapproving as ever. But she would never let Nancy see what she really felt.

Apart from Roderick, the hotel had no guests, so the aunts were free to make leisurely preparations for their day out, for of course, they were invited.

Roderick too would be among the guests. Nancy had made a point of inviting him herself. She was sure it would please Elvina.

Elvina was to be chief bridesmaid, with Daisy as the other attendant. They had gone with Nancy to choose dresses at a department store in Truro.

It had been a delightful day out. Daisy had been in a high state of excitement as they waited for the bus.

'I've never had a bought dress before,' she kept saying.

Elvina, for whom this wasn't an unusual occurrence had smiled at her indulgently. 'I hope Zed will find somewhere to take you afterwards so that you can wear it again,' she said.

Nancy had already bought her dress, but no one, not even her bridesmaids, had seen it. She had gone by train to London to stay with her Aunt Olive, and had been taken to a very grand store to choose it.

Mr Corey had insisted on paying for all the dresses. They were presents for Elvina and Daisy, who were determined to do him proud.

On arrival in Truro, they had gone

straight to the department store. Elvina, who had visited it before with her aunts, led the way.

Dresses were on the third floor. Daisy stepped fearfully into the lift behind the other two, determined not to show that she was terrified. It was the first time she'd travelled in a lift. She breathed a sigh of relief when they stepped out. Her eyes widened when she saw the rails of dresses.

Nancy selected a friendly looking saleslady and explained their mission.

'How exciting,' said the saleslady, 'had you any particular colour in mind?'

Nancy pointed to her friends' hair. 'Something to suit them both,' she said.

'There's always blue. That seems to suit everyone.'

'I'd like — peach,' said Daisy suddenly. They looked at her in surprise.

'I saw a film,' said Daisy, dreamily, 'where a girl wore a peach dress to a dance. She had peach shoes too. She looked lovely.'

Elvina and Nancy looked at each other then at the saleslady. 'I'll see what we have,' she said, and disappeared.

'I'm so sorry,' said a crestfallen Daisy to Elvina. 'You're chief bridesmaid, you should choose. Perhaps you don't like peach.'

Before Elvina could reply, the assistant was back bearing two dresses in softest peach. 'These only came in yesterday,' she said excitedly. 'I must say, they're very pretty.'

The dresses had little lace sleeves and a bow of peach satin ribbon at the base of the neck, with ends which reached almost to the hem.

'Oh-h-h.' Daisy put out a hand and tentatively touched a dress. She was obviously imagining herself wearing it.

Nancy looked at Elvina. 'I like them. What do you think?'

'Shall we try them on?' The girls followed the saleslady to the fitting-room at the back of the shop.

Five minutes later, two peach-clad girls were pirouetting excitedly in front of Nancy. The long slim style suited them both.

'We could dye white satin shoes to match the dresses,' offered the saleslady.

The girls looked at each other, nodded simultaneously and burst into laughter. The saleslady joined in and whisked the dresses away to be carefully packed in tissue paper and sturdy bags.

Elvina conducted her friends to the restaurant on the top floor where they discovered they were not too excited to eat iced cakes and drink coffee.

'May we look around the shop afterwards?' asked Daisy. 'I've never been anywhere like this before. It's a dream. It's like you see in the films.'

That had been a week ago and now, after breakfast, Elvina went to her bedroom and took the peach dress from the wardrobe.

She brushed and brushed her hair till it shone, then lifted a tress from each side and fastened it at the back with a peach coloured silk rose. Carefully she drew on the silk stockings the Aunts had bought for her. She must be very careful not to ladder them. They were expensive and would be her 'best' ones for a long time.

At last she lifted the peach dress from the hanger and slipped it over her head. It slithered down her body, fitting perfectly. She looked at her reflection in the long mirror on a stand and sighed with pleasure.

There was a knock at the door. Daisy, as ready as she was, had come down from her attic room. They stood, side by side, admiring their twin reflections in the mirror.

'Just wait till they see us,' breathed Daisy.

'Who?' Elvina looked at her.

'Zed and Mr Landry of course.'

'Oh Daisy. Don't make me blush. It doesn't suit my dress.'

Daisy laughed. Then she pointed at the window. 'Look! Sun! The mizzle's gone. It's going to be a lovely day.'

It was true. While she dressed. Elvina

had failed to notice the change in the weather. Now the sun shone, palely at first, but with the promise of brightness to come. A thought came into her mind. 'Happy the bride the sun shines on.' The sun would shine on Nancy and she would be happy. She would be happy with her Mr Bun.

The girls went downstairs. Roderick was waiting in the lounge with the aunts. They were smart too; Aunt Susie in a cherry coloured dress and Aunt Tilly in navy. They both wore new hats with cheerful ribbon decorations.

Roderick stood up to greet the girls. 'What a beautiful pair of bridesmaids,' he said, but his eyes were on Elvina.

'The car will be here soon,' said Aunt Tilly. 'Here are your flowers and she handed a small posy of cream roses tied with a peach ribbon, to each girl.

Mr Corey had ordered cars to take the guests, first to the village church, then along the cliffs to the Smugglers' Rest Hotel.

Nancy was waiting for them in the

porch of the church. She looked splendid in her bridal gown, as elegant as a fashion model. The gown was a column of white satin with two embroidered panels which hung from the shoulders, forming a train. She wore a gauzy veil held low on her forehead by a diamanté band. Her hair was hidden beneath the veil.

'Nancy, you look wonderful,' said Elvina.

'Like a film star,' breathed Daisy.

'And you both look beautiful,' said Nancy, taking Zed's arm. He was to give her away. 'I think we should go. The organ has begun to play.'

They walked slowly behind her down the aisle. I can't believe this, thought Elvina. Nancy getting married and looking so grown-up.

When will I get married? And who will I marry? As the thought entered her mind, she caught sight of Roderick gazing at her. What if I married Roderick? What if I was walking down the aisle towards him, in a beautiful white dress. The idea sent colour flooding into her cheeks and she hastily looked up at the barrel vaulted roof and tried to concentrate on the ceremony.

They'd reached the altar. Eli was waiting in very formal dress, with an equally short best man. Oh dear, thought Elvina, suppressing an urge to giggle. When she thought of Mr Bun in his apron and baker's hat, she had to lower her head and bite her lips.

'What's wrong?' hissed Daisy.

Elvina shook her head. 'Nothing.' She concentrated on taking Nancy's bouquet of white irises and checking her train, until she had composed herself.

I'm a silly, frivolous girl, she told herself severely. Roderick wouldn't want to marry me. I had better accept Jack — he and I have the same silly sense of humour.

Jack and Clay were ushers, looking very strange in their formal suits. Elvina looked down to see if Jack was wearing his seaboots. There I go again, she thought, feeling laughter bubble up. What is to become of me?

At last the service was over. Nancy was Mrs Eli Corey and Elvina with Jack, and Daisy with Clay followed the happy pair down the aisle.

'What about it then?' asked Jack.

'What about what?'

'Me and you next. A wedding.'

'No thank you.'

'I hope you haven't got your eye on that foreigner. He won't suit you. I've told you before.'

They'd reached the door. Everyone was lining up for the photographs which Elvina knew from experience would take ages.

Elvina left Jack and went to stand beside Nancy. 'I hope you'll be so happy,' said Elvina, kissing her friend.

'I know I shall be,' said Nancy firmly.

Elvina would have liked to sit next to Roderick at the wedding breakfast but as a bridesmaid, she was at the top table. Roderick had been placed at the bottom, next to a cousin of Eli's. Elvina was pleased to see that she was a very plain girl.

When the meal and the speeches were over, Elvina and Daisy helped Nancy to change into her going away clothes, a wine red suit with a fashionable cloche hat decorated with tiny feathers.

'Are you going to tell us where you're spending your honeymoon?' asked Daisy, 'or is it still a secret?'

Nancy, obviously thrilled, took a deep breath. 'We're catching a train to London.'

They looked at her with new respect. London!

'We shall go to theatres and restaurants,' said Nancy. 'Eli has been before several times and he knows just where to take me.'

Elvina stared at her. Theatres and restaurants. Was this her friend Nancy, her childhood friend who'd always enjoyed the simple pleasures of the village and the coast. I've lost her, she thought. Our friendship will never be the same again.

Nancy looked at her little gold wristwatch, a present from her new husband, and picked up her bag. 'The train goes in half an hour,' she said, 'we should be leaving.'

'Don't forget your bouquet,' Daisy reminded her, 'you have to throw it.'

They left Nancy at the top of the stairs and joined the small crowd below. There was a gasp as Nancy appeared looking very smart and grown-up. She threw the bouquet high in the air. Daisy reached for it but it fell neatly into Elvina's hands. She looked up to see Roderick, opposite her, smiling gently.

'You see, you're next,' he said.

'That's right,' Jack flung an arm round her waist. 'Elvina's next. Elvina and me.' He pulled her out to the entrance of the hotel to watch the bridal couple drive away.

'Jack! I wish you wouldn't do that!' Elvina angrily pulled herself away from him.

'Do what?'

'You know what.'

'Take you away from your admirer? You're not for him.'

'You were pleased enough when he helped to rescue Johnny,' she reminded him.

'Yes, well . . . '

From the corner of her eye Elvina saw Roderick walking round the side of the hotel to where the cars were waiting. He had left his car with the others.

She ran after him. 'Roderick! Wait!'

He turned slowly. His face was expressionless. She felt a pain in the pit of her stomach.

'Don't look at me like that,' she said. 'I can't help Jack's nonsense.'

He took her hands. 'I'm in the way. You belong here with your friends.'

'No,' she protested. 'Of course I belong here, but friends have no right to tell me what to do. I want to . . . I want to be with you.'

Appalled for the moment, she realised what she'd said. She held her breath.

He gazed deep into her eyes, then he lifted her hands to his lips and kissed them. 'Will you let me take you out to dinner tomorrow?'

'Oh yes,' she breathed.

'But there's one condition. You must look just as you do now in that dress and those pretty shoes.'

'Agreed,' she said rapturously. 'I should like to wear them again, anyway. Where shall we go?'

'It will be a surprise. Do you think your aunts will allow you to go?'

'You ask them. Aunt Susie has a weak spot for you, especially when you help her pod the peas.'

He joined in her laughter. 'Now you must go back to your aunts and I shall go down to the cottage. There's still lots to do.'

'I wish I could come with you.'

He took her by the shoulders and turned her in the direction of the hotel. 'Off you go. I'll see you tomorrow.'

Slowly, without a backward glance, Elvina returned to the hotel. 'Where have you been?' asked Aunt Susie. 'It's time to go home.'

'Just for a little walk. I needed some fresh air.' Her aunt gave her a curious look, but said nothing. All the way home, Elvina hugged to herself the thought of the following evening.

★   ★   ★

The aunts gave permission for Roderick to take Elvina out to dinner. Perhaps they felt she was missing Nancy and needed a little treat. Elvina blessed the day she'd had the idea of suggesting that Daisy should come and help at the hotel. It made it much easier for her to evade some of her duties.

Daisy had settled in well and was a great help. There was talk of her continuing to work part-time when she was married.

In her bedroom, Elvina once again took the peach dress from the wardrobe. She thought that the hairstyle she had adopted as a bridesmaid was not quite the thing for dinner. So with Daisy's help, she contrived a more elegant chignon at the nape of her neck.

Roderick surveyed her critically when she came downstairs to join him. 'Yes, almost the same. But what about the hair?'

'Don't you like it?' she asked anxiously.

He hesitated for a moment before breaking into a smile. 'It's lovely. Makes you look like a Greek statue.'

'I hope I'm not as cold as a statue.'

'I'll find out some time,' he promised, and wrapping her stole around her shoulders, led her out to the car.

★ ★ ★

Chequers Hotel did not look out to sea but stood on rising ground a few miles inland. It was surrounded by a beautifully laid out garden which they drove through before parking at the foot of a flight of granite steps.

They mounted the steps and passed

under a portico into a black and white foyer. The floor was laid out in a chequered pattern. The furniture and decorations were polished black and startling white. Couches upholstered in deep crimson and velvet curtains of the same shade were the only relief.

They were led into the dining-room. Here the same black and white theme prevailed, but the contrast was a rich peacock blue. As she sank onto a comfortable velvet chair, Elvina was glad that this was not the crimson room. She was sure her dress looked well against the peacock blue.

She looked around the room with pleasure. 'What a startling hotel.'

'It's very modern,' agreed Roderick. 'It was an old hotel before the war, very conventional, but it was bought by a Swedish builder with advanced ideas. It's only been open for two months.'

'How did you hear of it?'

'Kitty Rawlings mentioned it.' He handed her a menu and studied his own. 'The food doesn't seem too startling,' he said. 'Can you see anything you'd like?'

'I can't resist smoked salmon,' she said. 'Could I have that?'

'I'll have the same. The lemon and cucumber dressing will be nice and fresh. What then?'

Elvina looked again at her menu. 'I don't have to think about that. Chicken. It's my favourite meat.'

'I think I'll have . . . ' he pondered. 'Venison. We didn't have that in the trenches. I feel entitled to luxurious food now.'

Their orders given and wine poured, they sat back and looked at each other.

'How do you feel now that Nancy is married?' he asked. 'Are you resigned to her husband?'

'Oh yes. It's happened now. I just want her to be happy.'

'Good girl. That's the way to look at it. When will she be back?'

'Next Saturday. They've only gone for a week. Mr Corey can't leave the business for too long.'

The smoked salmon arrived. Elvina nibbled at her wafer thin brown bread and butter. 'Delicious! I wish the aunts would serve smoked salmon but it's too expensive for our hotel.'

'The food is excellent at your hotel,' he said. 'Do you do any of the cooking?'

'Not for guests, but I'm learning by practising on the aunts.'

He smiled. 'Perhaps I could try some of your cooking one day.'

'I don't think Aunt Tilly would allow that. She says I'm not ready to be let loose on the guests.'

'Perhaps you could cook something for me at Spindrift Cottage.'

Before she could answer, their main courses arrived.

'You mentioned the trenches just now. You haven't done that for some time. Are the memories beginning to fade?' Elvina asked.

'I don't think they'll ever disappear but they get a little easier to bear.'

'Perhaps you'll start painting soon,' she ventured.

He made no reply but shook his head slightly and continued with his meal. Elvina thought she'd better say no more on the subject.

'Would you like to dance?' Roderick asked when they'd finished eating, 'or would you like a dessert?'

'I'd love to dance.' Elvina was on her feet in a minute.

Roderick was an excellent dancer as Elvina had felt he would be. She was less accomplished. Her only dancing had been at the village dances with Jack and Clay, but she wasn't too disappointed by her efforts.

They danced on in silence. Elvina enjoyed the sensation of being in his arms, firm arms that held her securely and whisked her around the floor in a way that Nancy's brothers had never managed.

At last they returned to the table. 'What shall we have now?' he asked.

Again Elvina consulted her menu. She had a sweet tooth so this selection was very important.

'A pavlova,' she decided. 'I love meringue and cream.'

Roderick settled for cheese. When the pavlova came, it was filled with soft rich berries as well as the cream. Elvina gave a sigh of pleasure as she picked up her spoon and fork.

'If we dance again, it will have to be a very slow dance,' she said. As she finished eating, the orchestra struck up, 'If you were the only girl in the world'.

'Your slow dance,' said Roderick rising to his feet and holding out his hand.

Three dances later, they returned to their table. Elvina wished the night could go on for ever. She had never felt so happy; so at one with another person. She knew she could never put her feelings into words, but when Roderick said, 'We dance very well together, don't you think?' she agreed ecstatically.

He ordered drinks. Elvina drank eagerly. 'Dancing makes you thirsty,' she said.

'That didn't last long.' Roderick gestured to the waiter for more drinks. 'It's a good thing you prefer orange juice to wine, or I might have to carry you back to the car.'

'I have a rehearsal tomorrow for the Festival of the Sea,' she told him, 'so wine wouldn't be a good idea. It's only a few weeks away.'

'Ah yes. You're the Queen, aren't you? And your — friend — is King Neptune.'

She failed to notice the cold tone in his voice. 'Yes,' she agreed. 'I'm glad Jack is King Neptune. We always have fun together.'

'So I've observed,' he said.

This time she looked at him. 'I've told you before, Jack is a childhood friend. And Clay, of course, but at school, Jack was always my special friend.'

'At school. What about now? Does he have a lady friend?'

'No, he doesn't.' She took a sip from her glass and looked thoughtful.

'I think he regards you as more than just a friend. I think he's in love with you.'

'That's just his nonsense.' She brushed the idea aside. 'Every so often he asks me to marry him. I can't imagine marrying Jack. We're more like brother and sister.'

Roderick sat back in his chair. 'Let's change the subject. I'm not really interested in King Neptune.'

'What about your painting?' she asked brightly. 'Have you done any lately?'

That didn't seem to cheer him up. 'No. I'm not ready. One day, perhaps, but not yet.'

'I have an idea,' she said. 'What if you were to teach me. You might begin to regain your own desire to paint.'

She recoiled as he glared at her. 'Are you trying to trick me?' he demanded.

'Trick you? Whatever do you . . . ?'

'Do you think that by getting me to teach you, you can force me to start again myself?'

'Well . . . wouldn't it be a good idea?'

He was breathing heavily. 'I shall decide when I want to paint again. I don't need anyone else to interfere.'

Elvina felt tears sting her eyes. Why had he suddenly become so cold?

'I think I'd like to go home now,' she said in a small voice.

He looked at her, then he took her hand and stroked the back with his thumb. 'Elvina, I'm sorry. I'm being a brute. I know you only want to help. I haven't spoilt your evening, have I?' His expression was anxious.

She shook her head. 'Of course not. It's been a wonderful evening.' But he had, if not spoilt the evening, put a slight frost on it. She stood up. 'May we go now? I'm quite tired.'

Jack Makes His Feelings Known

'And this is my kitchen.' Nancy opened a door and Elvina followed her into a room. A large range dominated one wall and opposite, stood a tall dresser covered with coloured china. 'Eli's first wife liked to collect coloured china,' said Nancy, unconcernedly.

In the centre of the room was a scrubbed table but the only chair was a comfortable, cushion-filled armchair near the range. Skipper was in possession.

Elvina looked around. 'Where do you sit at mealtimes?'

'Oh we don't eat in here, we have a dining-room,' said Nancy proudly.

'And here is the parlour.' She opened another door. 'We don't keep it for best. Eli likes us to sit in here in the evenings.'

'What do you do in the evenings?' asked Elvina. 'You must miss your family.'

The room was crowded with old-fashioned furniture and dark green plants, but it had a large fireplace and looked as if it would be very cosy in the evenings.

'I read and sew, and I have some jigsaw puzzles.'

'What are jigsaw puzzles?'

'Oh they're great fun. We bought them in London. I'll show you later. And do look at what Eli has bought me.' An excited Nancy led her to a table in the corner. On it stood a box with a strange horn protruding from the top. 'It's a gramophone.' Nancy laughed at the bewilderment on her friend's face. 'Listen.'

She wound up a handle at the front and immediately the room was filled with wild, pulsating music. Startled, Elvina jumped at the first notes, but soon began to rock from side to side to the beat of the music.

'It's called jazz,' said Nancy. 'It comes from America. Come on, dance with me.'

They were still dancing when Eli Corey arrived home from the bakery. Embarrassed, Elvina stopped dancing, but Nancy continued to whirl about the room. Elvina watched her in amazement. Was this her quiet serious friend? Marriage had certainly changed her.

Nancy gave Eli a kiss. 'I'll make some tea,' she said and hurried out of the room. Eli gazed after her, fondly, then he turned to Elvina.

'I'm so pleased you've called to see her,' he said, making himself comfortable in a fireside armchair and gesturing to the girl to do the same. 'Please come as often as you like. I'm afraid she'll be lonely — coming from a large family and so on.'

Nancy returned with a tea tray. 'Our latest,' she said, putting a plate of cakes on the table. 'Coconut.'

'What did you think of London,' asked Elvina. 'Did you see everything?'

'I should think we did — Buckingham Palace, the changing of the guard, Kensington Palace — and we went on a river cruise.'

'Don't forget the theatre,' prompted Eli.

'We went twice,' said Nancy. 'We saw a murder and a comedy. It was so funny.' She and Eli smiled at each other, enjoying memories of their trip.'

And I thought she wouldn't be happy with him, Elvina thought reproachfully. She's glowing with happiness.

Later, when Elvina got up to go, Nancy stood up too. 'I'll walk a little way down the road with you,' she said.

They strolled slowly, arm in arm, back towards the village. 'I don't need to ask if you're happy,' said Elvina.

Nancy gave a sigh. 'I wish you could find someone to marry and be as happy as me,' she said, simply. 'What about your Roderick?'

'I told you before, he's not my Roderick. In fact, at this moment, he's Kitty Rawlings' Roderick.'

'What do you mean?'

'He's gone to stay at Penhallow Hall for a week or two. Kitty's brother, Ralph, is coming for a holiday. He and Roderick were brother officers in the war. Roderick wants to see him again.'

'And Miss Rawlings is still there?'

'I suppose so. I haven't heard that she's gone.'

Nancy gave her friend's arm a squeeze. 'I shouldn't worry. I'm sure he prefers you.'

*   *   *

In the morning, Elvina set off to do some marketing for her aunts. Before she was halfway down the hill, the rain, which had threatened at breakfast time, began in earnest.

Why didn't I bring an umbrella? She wondered whether to dash back to the hotel.

Suddenly there was a beep of a motor horn and a long black car drew in beside her. 'Jump in, Elf. I'll take you where you want to go.' It was Clay. 'Where would you like to go?'

'I'm only going to the shops.' She looked around. 'This isn't your car.'

'We've been working on it. I'm giving it a run to see if there are any more problems. Beauty, isn't she?'

'It's very nice. Not as nice as your little car, of course,' she said, loyally.

'Would you like a run? I'm only going a few miles along the coast road, but I'd be glad of the company.'

'I'd love it. But we mustn't be too long.'

'Right. Off we go.' Clay started the engine and they were soon speeding along. I'm getting quite used to driving in cars, thought Elvina, feeling very much a woman of the world.

'I heard the rehearsal for the Festival went well,' said Clay. 'Jack's really pleased.'

'Wait till you see my dress. Aunt Susie has finished it now. It's beautiful.'

'I wish I was King Neptune with you,' said Clay, wistfully, 'but I wouldn't like to have everyone looking at me.'

'You're not a show-off like Jack.' Elvina gave a little laugh. 'He loves to be looked at.'

'Will you save me some dances in the evening?'

'Of course.' She linked her arm with his for a moment.

'Elf, you know how I feel about you,' Clay began.

'Please, Clay, don't say any more. You and Jack are my best friends, but I've told you before, it can never be any more than that.'

He gave her a grin. 'I thought you'd say that, but it was worth a try.' He turned off away from the sea. 'Here we are again, back in the village.'

'Drop me at the garage,' said Elvina. 'I can walk up to the shops. It's stopped raining.'

The garage was close to the centre of the village. Clay pulled onto the forecourt and stopped.

'Come in and have a look round,' he

invited. Though she passed the garage several times a week, she had never been inside, so she accepted readily.

On the threshold she stopped, fascinated and appalled by the chaos. Bicycles, car tyres and buckets hung from bars across the ceiling. Tin advertisements for Esso and Castrol oil, Dunlop tyres and Exide batteries covered the walls.

In the centre was an old car, its bonnet raised, waiting to be worked on. Work benches around the wall bore a range of mysterious looking tools. Batteries, lanterns and metal buckets covered every available spot.

'However do you find anything?' she asked with a laugh.

Clay looked around, bewildered by the question, then he too laughed. 'We do all right. We have no women to tidy up. If we put something down, it stays there till we need it again. No one to put it away. Come and see the office.' They walked towards a door in the corner of the garage, but before they could reach it, it opened. Three men came out. One was the owner of the garage, Mr Millar, one was a stranger and one was Roderick.

Elvina stopped. 'Roderick. I thought you were at Penhallow Hall.'

The garage owner said goodbye, shook hands with the two men and went back into his office.

'See you again, Elf,' muttered Clay, and giving the others a quick salute, followed his employer into the office.

'Elvina. What a strange place to find you,' said Roderick.

'Clay gave me a lift because of the rain,' she said, not wanting to mention the ride along the coast road.

'This is Ralph Rawlings. Ralph, my friend, Elvina Simmons. She lives at the hotel where I'm staying.' The two shook hands. Ralph Rawlings was a tall, wiry young man with short curly brown hair and a friendly smile.

'We're looking round a few garages,' Roderick explained. 'We have an idea for the future.'

'I believe you mentioned it,' said Elvina as they walked towards the door. 'You'd like to open a garage yourself.'

'I had a lot to do with vehicles in the war,' said Ralph. 'The idea of a garage appeals to me too. Profitable business these days, I should think.' The partner Roderick mentioned, I suppose, thought Elvina.

'I've got my old bus outside,' said Ralph. 'Can we drop you anywhere, Miss Simmons?'

'Bus?' she queried.

The men laughed. 'He means car,' explained Roderick.

'No, thank you. I have some shopping to do for the aunts,' said Elvina, 'in fact, I'd better hurry. They'll wonder where on earth I am.'

Both men gave a little bow and Elvina hurried out of the building and up the road towards the grocer's shop.

Two women were waiting to be served when she entered Mr Penn's shop. Elvina's heart sank. Mr Penn never let a customer go without a good gossip. She'd be unable to get away quickly.

She gazed round the shop. Every inch was packed with something to buy Blocks of cheese covered in hessian sacking; large tins of biscuits and blocks of butter. Cards of buttons and shoelaces; bloomers and Liberty bodices. Ironmongery hung from hooks in the beams.

Shelves were piled high with tins of food and bars of chocolate and against the wall were stout boots and tins of paraffin.

At last it was her turn. Mr Penn bent over the sack of sugar and filled the brown paper bag with his scoop. He did it slowly, being careful not to spill a grain. Elvina fretted with impatience.

When at last she had her purchases and was on her way back to the hotel, she had time to think about Ralph Rawlings. Not much like his sister — friendly, and not inclined to look down his nose at a girl who lived in a hotel. A nice friend for Roderick, she thought approvingly.

But what about Kitty? Was she still there? The men hadn't mentioned her. Perhaps she'd returned to London. Please let her have returned to London, well away from Roderick.

* * *

Roderick returned to the hotel two weeks later. The aunts remarked to each other how Elvina's spirits seemed to rise, but said nothing to her. Daisy, less discreet remarked the next day, 'You seem in a happier mood, I must say.'

'Happier mood?'

'Yes. Real grouchy you've been lately.'

'I have not!' Elvina flushed.

'Oh yes you have. But you'll be more cheerful now Mr Landry's come back.'

Elvina glared at her. 'You'd better fold those napkins again, they look a mess,' and she flounced out of the room.

But she was happier. To see him at his usual table at breakfast made her want to smile all day. After the encounter at the garage, she hadn't seen him till he returned to the hotel. She'd missed him.

'What about another game of tennis this afternoon?' he asked on his first day back. 'Will you be free?'

They set off at two. The afternoon was fine; not a cloud in the sky.

'I've booked a court,' he said, 'we can go straight in.'

Of course he beat her easily once again, but Elvina didn't mind. It was enough to be with him. She had to work hard to give him a decent game but he seemed satisfied.

'Well played, partner,' he said as they mounted the stairs to the tearoom.

'You're being kind,' she said. 'I'm no better than last time. And I was pretty bad then.'

They chose a table, sat down and Roderick ordered tea and cakes. 'Did you play much tennis at Penhallow Hall?' she asked.

'Actually I did. Most days. Ralph is very keen.'

'Did you just play with Ralph?' She dreaded that he would say he's played with Kitty.

'No.' He took a cake while she waited for his reply. 'They had two tennis parties while I was there. I played with lots of people. That's why I beat you,' he said kindly. 'I've had plenty of practice.'

'And Ralph's sister?' she couldn't stop herself asking.

'Kitty went home, rather under a cloud.'

Elvina looked at him for a moment, then forcing herself to speak, unconcernedly, she repeated, 'Under a cloud?'

Roderick sighed. 'In a way, it was my fault, yet it righted a wrong. I was sitting in an armchair one evening when I dropped a coin. We'd been sorting pennies for a game. The coin seemed to have dropped down the side of the chair. I pushed my fingers down to see if I could feel it, when I felt something small and hard. I eased it out and found it was a ring.'

Elvina was watching him closely and her mind began to race ahead. A ring!

'I held it up. Kitty took it from me and said, 'That looks like the one I lost a few weeks ago. So that wretched girl didn't take it after all'.'

Wretched girl! Daisy!

'So what happened?'

'Lady Crace came across and took it from her. She looked at it for just a minute then she said, 'You know it's yours, Kitty. It belonged to your mother. I remember it well'.'

'Kitty looked a bit shamefaced then she took the ring and put it on her finger. Lady Crace said, 'What are you going to do about it?' Kitty looked at her as if she hadn't an idea what she meant, but I think she was playing for time. She said, 'Do about what?'

Lady Crace began to get impatient. She said, 'Do about the girl, Daisy. You caused her to be dismissed.'

I began to feel very uncomfortable listening to the argument so I made some excuse and left the room.'

'So you didn't hear what happened next. What she intended to do about Daisy?'

'No, but Kitty went back to London the next morning. She didn't wait for her brother. I think she wanted to leave as soon as possible.' He looked at Elvina with a frown. 'Is Daisy the young girl I see about the hotel occasionally — small, with a timid look?' He slapped a hand against his forehead. 'Of course — she was Nancy's other bridesmaid. She looked so different.'

'Yes. She's engaged to Zed, Nancy's oldest brother. I asked the aunts to take her on here until she marries. She needs money for her wedding.'

'I see,' he said, thoughtfully.

'I can tell you what happened,' said Elvina. 'Lady Crace came to the hotel to see Daisy.'

'To the hotel?'

'Yes. She asked to see Daisy alone, but Daisy was shy — or frightened. So I went with her. Lady Crace told us what had happened. She said that she was very sorry, that she'd missed Daisy and even asked her to return to the Hall in her old position.'

'What did Daisy say?'

'She thanked Her Ladyship but said she was getting married soon and was very happy here. Then Lady Crace took something from her bag and handed it to Daisy and said that it would help with her wedding clothes and that she hoped she and Zed would be very happy.'

Elvina looked around to make sure that no one could hear and whispered, 'Twenty pounds! She gave her twenty pounds!'

Roderick smiled at the look of awe on her face, then he said, 'Well that certainly was very kind.'

Elvina nodded and picked up the teapot. 'Lady Crace didn't say that you had found it. Once again you've helped someone in Nancy's family.'

'It was an accident.' He passed his cup and she poured carefully. 'It was bound to be found some time.'

'So Daisy and Nancy and I are off to buy a wedding dress for Daisy. We're going to Penzance this time.'

'And shall you be a beautiful bridesmaid again?'

'Daisy wants children for her attendants. That seems right for her somehow. She's like a child herself.' Elvina gave a gentle smile.

'When shall you go to Penzance?'

'The day after tomorrow. We'll get a bus after breakfast.'

'And the wedding will be . . . ?'

'Next weekend. They want all the village to come. Aunt Susie has made a huge wedding cake and there'll be sandwiches and pies and little cakes and jellies. The food will be in the church hall and in the evening there'll be dancing in the square.

'Quite different from Nancy's wedding.

'Yes. Isn't it strange, we haven't had a wedding in the village for months and now we have two close together.' She looked up to find him giving her a strange look. She flushed.

'What's wrong? Why are you looking at me like that?'

He seemed to come to with a start. 'I'm sorry. I was just thinking what a lovely bride you'd make.'

'Me? I don't think I shall be a bride for ages.' Confused, she gathered up her bag and tennis racquet. 'May we go now? It's getting late.'

★　★　★

Soon after breakfast two days later, Nancy appeared at the hotel and soon the three girls were on a bus on their way to Penzance. Elvina was glad to see that Nancy wore a simple cotton dress as in the old days. She was one of them again.

'I know where I want to go for my dress.' Daisy took a piece of paper from her pocket and studied it. 'Annie Kent told me about it. See, this is the name of the shop.'

'There are two department stores in

Penzance,' said Nancy. 'Why don't you look there first?'

'I don't want department stores,' said Daisy, firmly. 'I don't want to spend all my money and they're expensive. Annie said they have lovely dresses in . . . ' she looked at the paper again, 'Country Modes, so we'll go there.'

Nancy took the paper. 'I know where the street is. It's this way. Come along, we'll soon find it.'

The shop was on a corner and quite easy to find. With the confidence she'd gained when shopping for her bridesmaid's dress, Daisy led the way and pushed open the door.

An elderly lady with grey hair in a bun and sharp features, stared at them over the counter. 'May I help you?'

'I would like a white dress suitable for a wedding,' Daisy said in a small voice.

'We don't sell wedding dresses,' said the elderly lady.

Daisy drew herself up to her inconsiderable height and said, 'I don't want a wedding dress, I want a white dress which would be suitable for a wedding.'

The shop owner stepped from behind her counter and advanced on the dress rails. She gave Daisy a considered stare, assessing her size, then pulled out three or four dresses. She handed one each to Elvina and Nancy and held up two herself. 'Do you like any of these?'

Daisy studied them. She took the one Nancy was holding. 'I'll try this on. Come with me, Elf, please.'

They were soon back, Daisy wearing the dress which was made of soft white cotton with flowers embroidered in white and pink on the skirt and round the square neck. She looked enquiringly at Nancy.

'It's not a wedding dress . . . ' Nancy began.

'I don't want a wedding dress,' Daisy cut in.

'It's not a wedding dress,' Nancy repeated, 'but it looks very sweet on you and will be just right for the sort of wedding you're having.'

'That's what I said,' Elvina agreed.

'I'll take it,' said Daisy, 'and I'd like some white satin shoes to go with it, please.'

Outside, carefully holding the bags, Daisy gave a sigh of satisfaction. 'Just what I wanted.'

★ ★ ★

'How would you like to come with me to choose some furniture for Spindrift Cottage?' Roderick asked Elvina next morning after breakfast.

'Oh how exciting. I should love it.' Then her face fell. 'But I couldn't be free until eleven o'clock. I must do my chores first. I can't leave everything to Daisy.'

'Of course,' he nodded. 'Eleven o'clock will be fine.'

Elvina raced through her morning chores. 'If you worked this fast every morning, you'd have more free time,' Aunt Tilly remarked drily.

226

Aunt Susie had given her permission to go with Roderick. Elvina didn't think she'd mentioned it to Aunt Tilly.

At a quarter past eleven, she raced upstairs to her bedroom and changed into a navy and white checked dress she had finished making a month ago and had been keeping for a visit to town.

'I thought you had furniture in store for the cottage,' she commented as they drove along.

'I have.'

'Then why are we going to buy some more?'

He turned his head quickly and gave her a smile. 'We're not. We're going out to lunch.'

'But you said . . . ' she began, then stopped. 'I see. It was an excuse.'

'I thought the aunts would be more likely to let you go if they believed you were helping me.'

She was silent. 'Don't you want to come to lunch?' he asked.

'Yes, of course. But I was looking forward to choosing furniture.'

'Never mind. After lunch, we'll choose some ornaments so that you can truthfully say you helped me.'

He took her to a tiny inn on the edge of Penzance. The choice of food was limited, but she thought their Cornish pasties the best she had ever tasted.

'I should have chosen somewhere grander,' he said regretfully. 'You look much too smart for a little place like this.'

'Why shouldn't little places have smart customers?' she asked, preening a little at his compliment. 'Anyway, I think it's a dear little inn.' She looked around the tiny 'snug' admiring the rows of Toby jugs hanging from the old blackened beams and the way the flames of the wood fire sent flickering lights on to the brass fender and firedogs.

They lingered over their meal then drove into town and parked the car.

'I think there are two antique shops in this street,' said Roderick. 'Let's go and see if anything appeals to you.'

228

The interior of the first shop was gloomy and cluttered and utterly fascinating. Elvina wandered around picking up ornaments. Suddenly she stopped in front of a large pottery pig, lavishly decorated in bright colours and with a slot in his back.

'I do like this,' she said to Roderick. 'Wouldn't it brighten up a room?'

Roderick picked it up and tucked it under his arm. 'First purchase,' he said. 'Find something else.'

Elvina continued her wanderings. 'This would be useful,' she said, pointing to a cast iron doorstop in the form of a sunflower.

Roderick bent to pick it up, grimacing at the weight. 'Find something lighter next,' he suggested.

'Let's try the other shop,' she suggested. Roderick paid for the doorstop and the pig and they took them to the car. Then they tried the second shop. The first thing Roderick noticed was a beautiful old silk rug in muted colours. He stroked the surface reverently. 'I'm sure this is quite old. It would look lovely in the cottage.'

'But the sand,' Elvina protested. 'You are so close to the beach. The sand would ruin it.'

'These rugs were used in tents in the desert,' he said. 'Sand shouldn't affect them.' He fingered the ticket on the end. 'My goodness! Perhaps you're right, I should look for something less exotic.'

'What about that brass jug for umbrellas and walking sticks,' suggested Elvina. 'It would look well just inside the door.'

'It would take a bit of cleaning to keep it as shiny as that.'

'For sixpence, Johnny or Isaac would do it for you.'

'Good idea. We'll take it. Anything else?'

'Well . . . ' she hesitated, 'there's a lovely chair in the other room. But you don't want furniture, do you?'

'Show me.'

She led the way to the small room

leading off the main shop. In a corner was a very low, well-upholstered chair in old pink and lilac chintz. 'Isn't it pretty?' Elvina sat in the chair looking up at her companion. He studied her, saying nothing.

'Well?' she asked anxiously. 'Do you like it?'

'You look so pretty sitting there it could have been made for you,' he said. 'We'll take it, and every time you come to the cottage, you must sit in it.'

'It will be my chair,' she agreed, happily.

'My furniture is arriving tomorrow,' he said as they drove back to the village. 'I've finished painting the walls and Mrs Banden has made the curtains and came yesterday to hang them.'

'And will you leave us and move into the cottage now?' she asked in a small voice.

He took her hand and pressed it. 'Not yet. I don't feel ready to branch out on my own yet.' He gave her a smile. 'It's nice to be waited on. When the furniture is in place, you must come down and arrange our new purchases.'

Elvina was silent, daydreaming. What if Spindrift Cottage was hers and Roderick's. What if she was arranging her new home. But Roderick might not even live in it. He might go back to the Midlands and let the cottage. Or even worse, he might return with a bride and Elvina would have to watch another girl take the place she wanted so much. She gave a little shiver.

'Cold?' he asked, giving her a quick glance.

'No. Just an unpleasant thought.'

Elvina decide to change the subject. 'It's Daisy and Zed's wedding on Saturday. You are coming, aren't you?'

'Certainly. It will be fun to experience a village wedding. Perhaps we can sit together this time as you're not bridesmaid.'

'And you'll dance with me?' She gave him a sideways look.

'Try to stop me. But I expect I'll have to join a queue.'

★   ★   ★

Daisy and Zed's wedding was in full swing. Everyone in the village had turned up, most bringing cakes or sandwiches to supplement the food provided.

Daisy, a picture in her white dress and circlet of flowers was bright and sparkling, quite unlike her usual quiet self. Zed, proud and happy, was content to follow her around like a besotted puppy.

'Doesn't she look happy,' he kept saying to everyone who stopped to congratulate him.

The ceremony and the food over, everyone got ready to dance in the square for as long as they had the energy. Braziers had been lit and gave a mysterious warm glow to the scene. The fiddlers tuned up, Daisy and Zed started the first dance and soon the square was a mass of whirling figures.

Elvina was afraid that Roderick would refuse to dance as he had before, but suddenly he was there in front of her, pulling her into the whirling crowd. The fiddlers played six dances without a break and Elvina and Roderick danced every one.

Clay was dancing quite happily with Jill Evans but Elvina couldn't see Jack. She had expected him to ask her for a dance, but he was nowhere in evidence and she soon forgot about him.

'I'm quite dry,' she said to Roderick, 'let's get a drink.'

Bottles and jugs and glasses were set up on a trestle table and they were soon enjoying long draughts of cold beer and lemonade.

Clay joined them with Jill. The schoolteacher was introduced to Roderick. He looked pleased that Clay had found himself a partner instead of hanging around Elvina.

The band struck up again. 'Do you want to dance again?' asked Roderick, 'or shall we go for a stroll?'

'I need to cool down,' she answered. 'Let's stroll down to the harbour.'

Slowly they walked away from the music and laughter towards the harbour. A full moon shone silvery above, catching the waves as they slowly turned over towards the shore. The bobbing boats below carried riding lights which shone like stars.

'The harbour looks quite magical,' said Elvina. Then on a rocky piece of ground, she stumbled and Roderick, clutching her, wrapped an arm round her waist for support.

They walked on, Elvina so happy that she couldn't trust herself to speak. If she did, Roderick would guess that this was the place she most wanted to be in all the world. My darling love, she whispered to herself. If only he could feel as I do.

Suddenly a figure loomed up in front of them. 'Take your arm away from her,' a voice said thickly. 'D'you hear me. Leave her alone!'

'Jack!' Elvina was shocked and frightened. She pressed closer to Roderick. Jack was obviously drunk and out of control. Elvina knew how strong he was and was fearful for Roderick. 'Jack, we're only going for a walk.'

Jack took no notice. He made a lunge at the other man to pull him away from the girl. As he did so, Roderick stepped to one side and Jack, off balance, fell forward, twisting his leg under his body. There was an audible crack and Jack let out a bellow of pain and clutched his leg.

'Let me see.' Roderick fell to his knees and attempted to ascertain the damage but Jack punched him in the shoulder. 'Get off!' he shouted. 'Get off! Get away from me!'

Roderick stood up. 'I'll stay here with him,' he said to Elvina. 'You run back and get help.'

The next hour was a nightmare for Elvina. Somehow she found Clay in the crowded square and explained what had happened. He collected a group of friends and together they carried Jack back to his cottage.

'We'll go round the back alleys,' Clay

decided, 'don't want to spoil the wedding party.'

Elvina accompanied them, walking beside the makeshift stretcher and holding Jack's hand. She didn't know what had happened to Roderick and couldn't leave Jack to find out.

When Jack had been handed over to his mother's care, Clay took Elvina back to the square.

'I'm sorry, Elf,' he said. 'Jack's a fool when he's had a drink. But he loves you so much he can't bear to see you with the foreigner.'

'But Clay, he isn't a foreigner,' she protested.

'He's not from here. He's not Cornish,' Clay said obstinately. 'He'll always be a foreigner to us.'

In the square, the party was over. Daisy and Zed had left to spend their first married night in the best room at the hotel. The aunts had insisted. Roderick was nowhere to be seen. Elvina helped to carry glasses to the church hall to be washed in the morning, then slowly made her way home.

'Would you like a mug of cocoa?' asked Aunt Susie, handing her a mug without waiting for an answer.

'Is Roderick back?' she asked.

'Yes. He came in half an hour ago.' They looked at her curiously. 'Did you two have a quarrel?'

Elvina looked at them, then realised that they knew nothing of what had happened. Only the young people had stayed in the square for the dancing.

Briefly she explained. 'But I don't want to discuss it now. I'm too tired. We'll talk in the morning.' She gave them a kiss and wearily climbed the stairs to her room.

What an ending to a lovely day, she thought. And what am I going to do about Jack? I can't love him, not as I love Roderick. Even if he goes away, I'll always love him. There can never be anyone else.

Roderick Makes Plans to Leave

The next morning, Roderick was the first down for breakfast so Elvina was able to have a few words with him.

'Have you heard anything of your friend?' he asked, shaking out his napkin.

She placed a basket of hot toast on the table. 'No. Daisy will have some news when she comes in.'

'Does he have to behave like that?' Roderick asked. 'I'm sorry, Elvina, I know he's your friend, but his behaviour is intolerable.'

'He's always been quick tempered,' she said, miserably. 'I'm sorry you were involved. I'm sure he'll feel dreadful when he realises it was all his fault.'

'He'll certainly have a thick head as well as a sore leg this morning.' said

Roderick, 'and I can't feel too sorry for him.'

When Daisy arrived she reported that the doctor had called and that Jack had a broken ankle. 'He won't be able to walk on it for weeks,' she said. 'He's in an awful temper because of course he can't work.'

A sudden thought struck Elvina. The Festival! How could he be King Neptune? What would happen now?

Clay answered that question when he called at the hotel later in the morning. 'They want me to be King Neptune now that Jack is out of it,' he said. 'I hate the idea.'

'Please, Clay, don't refuse. I'll feel so much better if you do it than someone I don't know.'

'I'm not Jack,' he said, bitterly. 'I don't like showing off and being looked at.'

'You'll be hidden behind a big flowing beard and long hair,' she said. 'Your face will hardly be seen. Please Clay.'

'Very well,' he said reluctantly, 'just for you, Elf. But I shall hate it.'

She flung her arms round him and gave him a kiss. He tried to grab her for another but she skipped away.

'We have to run through it this afternoon,' he said, 'though I'm sure it's quite easy. You can tell me what to do. Thank goodness we don't have to say anything. I'll call for you at two if you like.'

Roderick came downstairs as Clay was going out of the door. 'What did he want?' he asked suspiciously. 'Why must there be two of them?'

Clay is no trouble. Elvina sprang to his defence. 'He's taking over Jack's role in the Festival. And he's been helpful to you about the garage, don't forget.'

Roderick held up a hand. 'Pax,' he said. 'Don't let's fight. I agree Clay isn't like his brother. I came down to ask you to come to the cottage this afternoon if you can. I want you to make a list of the things I'll need to make the kitchen workmanlike.'

'I can't. What a pity. I should love to help, but I have to run through the Festival with Clay. He's not sure what to do.'

Roderick didn't bother to suggest another time. He gave a curt nod and left the hotel.

Clay picked her up in his little car at two o'clock and they drove to the church hall. 'This won't take long,' said Jill Evans, the organiser of the Festival. 'Thank you, Clay, for helping us out.'

She's sweet on Clay, thought Elvina, watching the other girl's eyes widen flirtatiously as she looked at Clay. Do I care? I don't think I do. I don't want Clay, so he should find someone else.

For half-an-hour, they went through the order of the proceedings. Clay had watched the Festival every year since he was a small child and it never differed, so it didn't take long to familiarise him with what he had to do.

'And you'll have Elvina with you all the time,' said Jill with a smile at the girl. She looked at Clay's solemn face.

'Cheer up, you'll enjoy it. And don't forget the party in the night.'

'We must have a lot of dances together,' said Clay to Elvina as they left the hall, 'because we're King and Queen.' He helped her into the car. 'We'll go to the garage and collect the shells. I've finished drilling them.'

Johnny had gathered a large bag of shells from the beach for Elvina and Clay was drilling holes in them so that she could use them to decorate her costume.

'He charged me sixpence, the little wretch,' she said with a laugh.

'I'll drop you off at the hotel,' Clay said when they'd called at the garage. 'Then I must get back to work. Mr Warren's been good at giving me time off so I mustn't take advantage.'

They had only gone a few hundred yards when Elvina spotted Roderick talking to a girl. 'Oh no.' Her remark was audible and Clay looked across at her.

'What's wrong?'

'Nothing,' she said hastily. 'I've just remembered something.'

Clay pulled up at the hotel and she jumped out with a word of thanks.

'See you at the hall tomorrow.' Clay gave her a wave and was gone.

Elvina walked slowly round the hotel to the kitchen door. Kitty Rawlings was back! Just when everything between her and Roderick was going well. It wasn't fair.

'There you are,' said Aunt Susie who was busy icing a cake in the kitchen. 'You'd better go and help Nancy comfort young Daisy. They're in the garden on the terrace.'

'Daisy? What's happened?'

'She and Zed have had a lovers' quarrel.'

'They'll have plenty of those,' said Elvina without much sympathy.

Daisy, eyes red-rimmed and face blotchy was sitting on the terrace nursing a beautiful silk scarf. Nancy sat opposite. She looked relieved when Elvina appeared.

Elvina sat down next to Daisy and waited for an explanation.

'It's this scarf,' Daisy began. Elvina took it from her. It was made of the softest silk in beautiful shades of pink, purple and lilac.

'It's gorgeous,' she breathed. 'Where did you get it?'

'Lady Crace sent it to me. It's from the silk works in Newlyn. The pattern is called . . . ' she looked across at Nancy.

'Abstract,' said Nancy. 'It's the very latest thing.'

Elvina handed back the scarf. 'But why are you upset I would think you'd be thrilled at such a gift.'

'Zed wants me to throw it away,' said Daisy with a hiccup.

'Throw it away!' Elvina was horrified.

'He says I shouldn't accept anything from them at Penhallow Hall after the way they treated me.'

'But that wasn't Lady Crace. When she realised what had happened, she came straight here to see you. And she gave you . . . ' She stopped, unsure whether to mention the twenty guineas.

'I didn't tell Zed about that,' Daisy admitted, her head lowered.

'Husbands don't need to know everything,' said Nancy, with the wisdom of a few months' marriage.

'Well I'm not throwing it away,' said Daisy defiantly. 'I've never had anything so beautiful.' She held the scarf to her chest with both hands.

'Put it away for a while and bring it out later when he's forgotten who gave it to you,' advised Elvina. She held out a hand to Daisy. 'Come on, let's go in and make a cup of tea.'

'And have some of the cakes I brought,' agreed Nancy.

'What brought you over?' asked Elvina, when they were sitting at the kitchen table. 'Aren't you helping at the bakery?'

'I only go in now and then,' said Nancy. 'Eli doesn't want me to work full time. I'll help this evening when he's getting the rolls ready for tomorrow.'

'Tomorrow,' said Elvina. 'Perhaps

Roderick won't want to come and watch. Perhaps he'll spend the day with Kitty Rawlings. And I so wanted him to see me in my lovely dress.'

'You don't sound very excited,' said Nancy. 'I thought you were thrilled to be the Queen of the Sea.'

'I am. It's just that . . . ' she stopped.

'What?'

'Kitty Rawlings is back.'

'And you're afraid he'd rather be with her,' said Nancy, summing up the situation. 'If he'd wanted to be with Kitty Rawlings, he'd have followed her to London. Now then, do you want me to come and help you dress tomorrow?'

Dear Nancy. So sensible. Elvina squeezed her arm. 'Of course I do. The aunts will be coming but they may not be able to leave the hotel early enough to dress me.'

'I'll be at the hall bright and early.' Nancy picked up her bag and pulled a new blue cloche over her dark hair. 'Must go now.' She patted Daisy's shoulder as she passed and called out a farewell to Aunt Susie.

When she'd gone, Elvina took the shells from her bag and gave them to Aunt Susie. Her aunt intended to sew them onto a belt for her waist and a circlet for her hair.

'I'd better go and wash my hair so that I can dry it in the garden,' she said. She was going to wear it loose and flowing the next day.

'I'll brush it for you when it's dry,' offered Daisy. She was over her crying fit. She folded the scarf carefully, put it back in its bag and placed it on the dresser till it was time to go home. 'I'll peel the potatoes now,' she said, going to the sink.

Elvina went upstairs. She wouldn't think any more about Roderick. There were more important things for the Queen of the Sea to think about.

★　★　★

Elvina was up bright and early. The aunts had packed her costume in a large flat box. At nine o'clock, Clay was at the door in his little car. Elvina climbed in and Clay placed the box on her lap. In ten minutes, they were at the church hall.

Nancy was waiting for her. The hall was buzzing with the excited chatter of the performers in the procession.

'Come and see your throne,' said Nancy, leading the way to the rear of the hall.

A large brown horse was being backed into the shafts of a farm wagon, but a farm wagon which had been transformed. It was covered with blue cloth and silver ribbons. On the cloth sat two thrones made of wood and painted silver. Cushions of silver cloth made them into comfortable seats. More silver cushions were scattered about the wagon.

The girls gazed at the magnificent equipage in silence. 'Well,' said Elvina at last, 'that's certainly fit for a king and queen.'

They went back inside the hall. 'By

the way, where's King Neptune? He seems to have disappeared. Poor Clay.' His sister laughed. 'He's not happy about his role. I think he'd gladly pay someone else to do it.'

They went into the tiny room allocated to Elvina as a dressing room. Nancy carefully lifted the sea-green dress from the box. 'Elf, it's beautiful,' she breathed.

An hour later, the procession was ready to move off. Everyone agreed that Elvina with her sea-green gauzy dress and long golden hair, made a beautiful queen. King Neptune in a purple tunic to his ankles, was completely hidden behind his beard and long grey hair.

On the scattered cushions sat six very excited small mermaids. Jill fussed around them, arranging their tails and smoothing their hair.

The first stop was the church. A crowd of children walked at the front of the procession followed by the village band. Then came the King and Queen on their thrones. Another crowd of villagers walked behind.

'Are you nervous?' Elvina whispered to Clay.

He nodded but said nothing. He'll be fine, she said to herself, smiling at him encouragingly. He'll enjoy it after a while.

King Neptune and his queen walked first into the church and took their seats at the front. Everyone else crowded in behind and filled the pews.

The singing was loud and enthusiastic. The minister gave a short address, reminding them of the story of the festival and the service was over. Everyone waited while the king and queen walked slowly out of the church and were helped again onto their thrones.

As they walked Elvina looked curiously at Clay. It must be his wig and his crown. Somehow he looked taller than usual.

They set off again through the village towards the harbour. The streets were lined with people who clapped and cheered. Many had come from nearby villages. The festival was very popular. Elvina waved elegantly, thoroughly enjoying herself.

'Remember what you have to do with your trident when we reach the harbour,' said Elvina. 'And for goodness sake don't drop it in the water. I don't expect they've got a spare.'

She turned to look at Clay and a tiny breeze blew his hair back from his face. She gave a gasp. It wasn't Clay.

'You've found me out,' said Roderick. 'Close your mouth, you look like a fish. It may be appropriate but it's not glamorous.'

'Where's Clay?' she asked, bewildered.

'In the church hall or the garage, or perhaps he's watching us from behind a tree. He couldn't face this, so I offered to do it for him. No one will know if I keep hidden behind this dreadful beard.'

Elvina began to laugh and couldn't stop. The crowd watching her thought

252

she looked so happy and beautiful, that they cheered more loudly. Roderick joined in the laughter and waved his trident.

They'd reached the harbour. Roderick climbed down with difficulty, nearly falling over his long tunic, and set off for the nearest boat. It was held steady as he climbed aboard and raising his trident, brought it down three times. This ceremony was repeated on each boat which was near enough to board.

Elvina, on her float, stood up and was handed a large bag. Inside were hundreds of little silver paper fish, laboriously cut out by the children at the Sunday school for weeks before. She tossed handfuls of fish in all directions and laughed as people scrambled for them. It was believed in the village that if you caught one, you would have luck all the year.

At last the fish were gone and Roderick joined her again.

'Phew,' he gasped, 'thank goodness that's over. I feel quite seasick. What now?'

They moved off again. 'The beach now.'

Crowds poured onto the beach and formed parties and family groups around white cloths laid on the sand. Bags and baskets were unpacked and soon everyone was enjoying a picnic meal.

King Neptune and the Queen of the Sea walked from group to group smiling and chatting. Roderick spoke as little as he could, but when he did, he had a strange almost Cornish accent.

'Why are you speaking like that?' Elvina hissed as they walked.

'I don't want to give Clay away so I'm trying to sound like him. Don't you like my accent?' He sounded hurt.

'You are throwing yourself into the part, aren't you,' she said. 'Look, there's the aunts and Nancy and Daisy. They'll have something for us to eat and drink. Come on.'

'Now I'm for it,' muttered Roderick. 'I won't be able to fool Clay's sister.'

But there was no need to try. Aunt Tilly gave him a stern look as he sat down on the sand.

'I don't think you're Clay,' she said, 'I think you're Mr Landry. What's going on?'

Explanations followed and were accepted. Everyone knew how shy Clay could be.

'But don't tell anyone,' Roderick begged. 'Clay will be at the church hall when we get back and we'll change over again.'

It was time to return to the village and for the last time the procession formed up again. Elvina thought she would remember being the Queen of the Sea for the rest of her life. Roderick held her hand as they rode back in style to the church hall.

Roderick disappeared to change and nobody noticed when, twenty minutes later, he and Clay strolled back into the main hall where Elvina was waiting.

Clay gave her a sheepish grin.

'Did you think I wouldn't discover?' she asked, severely. 'And what about Jill?'

'I've confessed. She's forgiven me. Don't be mad, Elf. I just couldn't do it when the time came. And anyway, Roderick asked me to . . . ' He stopped as he caught the other man's eye.

'Asked you to what?'

'Well, asked me to . . . ' Clay floundered.

'All right. I asked him if he'd like me to stand in for him,' said Roderick. 'I wanted to be in the procession with you, not stand at the roadside and watch you pass.'

'I must be off,' said Clay as if anxious to avoid what might be an argument. 'I'll see you this evening.'

'You're not really mad at me, are you?' asked Roderick in a wheedling tone. 'We had fun, didn't we? And I didn't make any mistakes.'

'What about Miss Rawlings?' The question was out before Elvina could stop it.

'Kitty Rawlings? What has she to do with anything?'

'I saw you with her this morning. I

passed you in Clay's car so you didn't see me.'

'Kitty came back to Penhallow Hall to collect her brother. They came down together in her car and when she went back to London after the incident with the ring, it left him without a car to drive home in. So she came back for him.

'I met her quite by accident when she'd taken a little drive down to the sea for a few sniffs of ozone. She wasn't staying.'

Elvina gave a sigh of relief. Roderick put an arm about her shoulders. 'You know I'd rather be with you than Kitty Rawlings, don't you,' he said softly. 'Come along, let's get your dress and I'll run you back to the hotel.'

* * *

When they returned some hours later, the hall was transformed. Bunting had been hung across from side to side, shells and seaweed decorated the

257

windowsills, and the thrones of King Neptune and his queen stood on one side of the stage facing the small band. During the evening, people would be allowed to take turns at sitting in them.

Roderick found a table and they were soon joined by Aunt Tilly and Aunt Susie, eager to observe the fun, though as Aunt Susie said, their dancing days were over.

'I learned some new dances at Penhallow Hall,' Roderick said to Elvina. 'I'll teach them to you if you like.'

'They wouldn't be much use here tonight,' she retorted. 'Can you see this lot,' she jerked her head towards the fiddlers who were tuning up, 'playing up-to-date dances?'

And who taught you, she wondered? Probably Kitty Rawlings. Well I don't care about Kitty Rawlings — she's in London and Roderick is here with me.

The music had started. Roderick stood up and held out his hand. 'Come on then. We'll do the old-fashioned dances.'

'This has been a wonderful day,' Elvina said as they glided around the floor. 'Almost perfect.' She sighed and stroked the back of his neck with one finger.

'For me too,' he agreed, 'thanks to Clay.'

'Poor Clay,' she said. 'He's so shy. I must have a dance with him. I promised, though I think he's quite happy at the moment.'

They looked across the room to where Clay, with Jill Evans in his arms, was gliding around the floor with unusual panache.

'I'll let him have one dance with you,' he agreed, 'but only one.'

They danced on in silence, each thinking back over the day. They had been joined on the floor by many more couples so there was less room. He held her closer.

'When I came down to Cornwall to find some peace after the last few years,

I never dreamt I'd find such friendship and happiness,' he said softly. 'You have been so sweet to me, even in the beginning when I was so awful.'

She smiled up at him, shyly. 'Not awful, just difficult. But I understood.'

'Awful and difficult,' he corrected. 'And I've received such kindness from your aunts. I almost feel I belong here.'

'You do belong here. You have Spindrift Cottage. It was handed on to you by your grandfather. You're not a stranger to this part of the world.'

He smiled down at her. 'My business will be in another part of the country, but Spindrift Cottage will always be here when I want to come back.'

'You're not leaving soon?' An icy feeling entered her heart.

'I can't stay much longer. Ralph and I have made plans. Things are beginning to move. We hope to open our garage in three months.'

The music stopped. Elvina stood still and looked at him. 'Where . . . where will it be?' she asked, faintly.

'In Worcestershire. On the edge of the city of Worcester. There's a large population, but plenty of countryside.'

Elvina began to walk towards their table. 'Countryside but no sea,' Roderick said as he took her arm. 'I'll have to come back to see the sea.'

'What will you do with the cottage?'

'Do? Nothing. It will just wait for me to return. You'll have a key and you can use it whenever you like.'

Elvina sat down opposite her aunts. 'I'll get some drinks,' said Roderick.

'You don't look very happy all of a sudden,' said Small Aunt. 'Has anything happened?'

'Roderick has just told me he will be leaving soon. He's starting a garage business in the Midlands.'

They looked at her with compassion, the Tall Aunt said, 'Well it had to happen. You knew he'd go some time.' Elvina knew they wanted to ask lots of questions but were too polite to do so.

Roderick returned with the drinks. 'They're starting to serve the food.

Shall we join the queue?'

Elvina felt she couldn't eat a thing but didn't want to draw attention to herself by saying that, so she stood up.

'Fuel for some more dancing,' said Roderick, putting an arm round her waist and leading her across the room to the food-laden tables.

Nancy and Eli were sitting at a large table with the Perrans family. Even Mrs Perrans had agreed to come for an hour or so. Jack sat with his leg up on a chair. He appeared not to notice Elvina and Roderick.

Elvina exchanged a little wave with Nancy but didn't stop to talk. She didn't want to get involved with Jack.

The band struck up again after the supper break. Before Roderick could claim her, Clay was standing by the table.

'You promised me a dance, Elf.'

Elvina smiled at Roderick and stood up at once. 'Of course,' she said, and they danced happily away. She didn't feel so happy when she passed Roderick dancing with Annie Kent.

I could hardly expect him to sit at the table while I danced, she thought, fairly. But she was glad when the dance with Clay came to an end and she was back with Roderick.

Ten minutes later, as they danced past the table where Jack was sitting, she felt her arm grabbed and she was pulled away from her partner.

'Come here, Elf. This is where you belong,' Jack shouted. 'Get back where you came from and leave my girl alone,' he bellowed at Roderick. 'Elf is mine. I love her. I've always loved her. I'm going to marry her.'

'Jack, please.' Elvina felt a deep blush suffuse her cheeks. 'Everyone is looking.'

'Let them look.' Jack was still holding her wrist.

'Leave me alone, you're hurting me.' She tried to pull free.

Luckily, Mrs Perrans had left before the embarrassing incident, so Jack was alone, but the rest of the family, hearing the noise, had come hurrying back.

Roderick stood, unsure what to do. His instinct was to attack Jack for hurting Elvina, but he couldn't strike an injured man. Clay came between them and quietened his brother. Nancy put her arm round Elvina and took her to sit at the far side of the table.

When Elvina had calmed down, she looked round for Roderick. He had vanished. Nancy took her back to her aunts.

'Where's Roderick?' she asked. 'Have you seen him?'

'No. He didn't come back here. Perhaps it's as well with Jack Perrans in that mood,' said Aunt Susie.

'He may have returned to the hotel,' suggested Aunt Tilly. 'We'll all stay a while longer then leave. Try to act as if nothing has happened.'

Elvina was quiet when they arrived back at the hotel. She refused a drink and went straight to her room.

She climbed into bed and before blowing out her candle, took a last look at her beautiful sea-green dress hanging on the back of the door.

Jack and his temper couldn't take away her lovely memories of the Festival. Tomorrow she would talk to Roderick and make him see that Jack would never be anything to her but a friend.

A Day That's Filled With Surprises

Elvina awoke the next morning to find the bedroom curtains outlined with golden sunshine. It was going to be another fine day. The clock said six-thirty. She stretched luxuriously. She'd had a good night's sleep.

Then she remembered. The dance at the church hall! Jack in a foul mood and Roderick puzzled and defensive. It was surprising she'd slept at all. She sat up. Perhaps Roderick would come down early for breakfast and they could talk.

She swung her legs out of bed. Carefully, she poured water from the jug into the china bowl on the corner table and welcomed the splash of cold on her face. It would help her to wake quickly.

She dressed, brushed her hair and tied it back and put on a clean white apron. Daisy would arrive later to help with lunch, so she had to help with breakfast.

The aunts were already in the kitchen eating their own breakfasts. They smiled at her warmly as she entered. They waited for her to speak, to introduce the subject of the dance last night.

At last she gave a rueful smile. 'I don't suppose you've seen Mr Landry.'

They shook their heads. 'He's probably still in bed,' said Aunt Tilly. 'Poor man. Jack Perrans was in a nasty mood.'

'It's not like Jack,' Aunt Susie said thoughtfully. 'He's usually such a sunny boy. It takes a lot to ruffle him like that. He feels strongly about something.' She looked at her niece.

Elvina finished her porridge and stood up, picking up a pile of clean tablecloths. 'I'll make a start on the breakfast tables,' she said. 'People may be down early.' He may be down early, she corrected herself. And if he is, I want to be waiting for him.

But Roderick didn't appear, neither early nor late. She went into the kitchen. 'He hasn't been down for his breakfast,' she said, dejectedly. 'Perhaps he's gone on one of his walks. Perhaps he was too fed up by the events of last night to face us.'

'He could be ill,' said Aunt Susie, doubtfully. 'Give him a little longer then we'll go up to his room.'

There was no reply to their knock on his bedroom door. Aunt Susie called his name discreetly but again there was no answer. With a sigh, she took a pass key from her apron pocket.

The room was tidy — and empty. All his belongings had gone from the bedside table and the dressing table. Elvina opened the wardrobe doors. Just empty coat hangers rattled together.

She collapsed onto the side of the bed. Tears began to run down her cheeks and she didn't care that her aunt was looking at her.

'He's gone and we didn't even talk,' she sobbed. 'He thinks I love Jack and I don't I love . . . I love . . .'

'You love him,' finished her aunt quietly. She sat beside the girl and put an arm around her shoulders. 'Or you think you do. He's the first man you've been friendly with, other than the Perrans boy. Do you think you saw more in your friendship than he wanted to give?' She handed a handkerchief to the girl who pressed it to her eyes.

'He was a stranger,' Aunt Susie said softly. 'We know very little about him or his family. He may even have had a sweetheart at home. Men sometimes say they love a girl just to . . .'

'He never said he loved me,' Elvina broke in quickly. 'Never. We didn't talk about things like that. But I loved him. I love him,' she corrected herself, 'and now he's gone.'

Aunt Susie glanced round the room and her eyes fell on a white envelope tucked behind a candlestick on the dressing table. She went across to pick it up and came back to the bed.

'It's addressed to Tilly and me,' she said. 'I'm sorry, Elvina.'

The girl didn't look up. 'He wouldn't even . . . even write to me,' she whispered.

Her aunt opened the envelope and scanned the contents. 'He thanks us for a wonderful stay and hopes he wasn't too much trouble,' she said with a thin smile. Then she extracted some notes and counted them. 'My goodness, how generous.'

'He doesn't mention me.' It was a comment not a question. Her aunt's arm tightened round her shoulders.

'I expect he'll write to you separately,' she said. 'It would be more private. Come along, we've got work to do. Keep busy and you won't feel so unhappy.'

Elvina worked hard for the rest of the morning, deliberately not thinking of Roderick.

When Daisy arrived, she began to talk about the evening before, obviously ready for a good gossip. Elvina stopped her.

'Mr Landry has gone,' she said, 'and I don't want to talk about him or last night.'

Immediately after lunch they had a visitor. Elvina, crossing the hall with water jugs in her hands, was surprised to see Mr Pensome, the nephew who had visited her with the brooch Granny Pensome had left her.

'Ah, Miss Elvina,' he greeted her. 'Do you think I could speak to your aunt for a few moments. Miss Mathilda Simmons,' he explained.

Elvina showed him into the lounge and went to find her aunt. Aunt Tilly had her arms immersed in soapsuds as she washed the lunch dishes, but she quickly rinsed and dried them, removed her apron and patted her hair in front of the small mirror on the wall.

Elvina was summoned to the lounge ten minutes later. Mr Pensome gave her a warm smile.

'We have some good news for you,

Miss Elvina,' he said. He looked at Aunt Tilly.

'I gave your brooch to Mr Pensome to get it valued,' Aunt Tilly explained. 'Here is the certificate.'

'The brooch contains some priceless emeralds,' Mr Pensome explained.

'These raise the value of the jewel way above what we would expect.'

Aunt Tilly handed the valuation certificate to Elvina. The girl studied it. Most of it was incomprehensible to her, but the large sum of money printed at the bottom was quite plain.

'You mean . . . you mean my brooch is worth all this?' she asked in amazement.

'Mr Pensome nodded. 'It is — if you want to sell it.'

Elvina looked at her aunt. 'We'll give the matter some thought, said the older woman, and I must discuss it with my sister, but I believe the best idea would be to sell it and invest the money for Elvina's future.'

Mr Pensome stood up. 'You know

where to contact me,' he said. 'Oh, I nearly forgot the brooch.' He reached into his waistcoat pocket and drew out the little box. 'Put it in your safe and let me know if you want me to sell it for you.'

Aunt Tilly saw him out. Elvina remained in her seat, thinking. So much money. She could help Roderick realise his dream of a garage. She could be a partner. Or, if he loved her as she loved him, and they married, she would help him as his wife.

Tears began to fill her eyes again and she bit her lip to stop them. What was the use of thinking like that. Roderick was gone. He wasn't interested in her. He hadn't even left her a letter. It was over.

She went slowly upstairs to splash cold water on her face. She'd walk over to see Nancy. She missed their carefree afternoons on the hill overlooking the sea. Nancy was a serious married woman now, even talking about having a baby. Elvina couldn't imagine Mr

Bun, as she still thought of him, with a baby, but Nancy insisted that he wanted one.

Elvina picked up her bag from the little dressing-table. As she did so, her eyes fell on a key on the pin tray. Spindrift Cottage! Roderick had had a key cut for her. What if he was there! How could she have forgotten the cottage?

It was decorated and almost completely furnished. He could be living there. Perhaps he meant her to think of it and meet him there. That was why he hadn't left her a letter.

Breathing quickly, she picked up the key and popped it into her bag. She ran downstairs, glad that no one was in the entrance hall. She didn't want questions about where she was going.

She hurried down the hill, not running, that would cause attention, but walking as quickly as she could.

She passed through the village and out onto the coast road. By now, she had convinced herself that he was waiting for her. A little smile played about her lips. 'I'm coming, my love,' she whispered. 'Just ten more minutes.'

The cottage looked deserted. A gull, hopping along the garden wall, rose into the air with a sharp screech and flew off across the waves. She opened the garden gate and hurried up the path and taking the key from her bag, inserted it quietly into the lock. I'll surprise him, she thought.

The silence hit her as she opened the cottage door. 'Roderick,' she called, uncertainly. She rushed through the living-room into the kitchen. It was empty. She flung open the back door. There was no one in the garden. Elvina had to acknowledge that the cottage was deserted.

She climbed the stairs with a heavy heart. She would look in the bedrooms but she knew he wouldn't be there.

Back in the living-room she moved to the window to look out at the sea. Silent tears began to course down her cheeks. He really had gone. Then, through her tears, she spotted the envelope on the window sill. She snatched it up and tore it open.

Dear Elvina, she read, *I've left this letter here so that you will be alone when you read it.* She backed towards her chintz armchair and sat down. *This evening has made me realise how I'm interrupting your peaceful life. Before I came, you were happy with your friends, Jack and Clay. I've taken you away from them and caused a lot of trouble.*

The scenes with Jack were very ugly but I don't blame him. He loves you and he resents me dreadfully.

My life is not in Cornwall, yours is. I cannot take you away from here. I want you to be happy as you were before I came.

We were friends — good friends, but I cannot offer you more than that. I haven't sorted out my life yet. My business will take all my capital, I cannot support a wife.

Being with you these past weeks has

given me the peace I was seeking. Now I must go forward carrying out the plans I've been making. My life will be insecure until I've established my business. It would be unfair to expect you to share that. And you've always said you'd hate to live away from the sea.

I haven't decided what I shall do with *Spindrift Cottage.* I may sell it or I may visit now and then. But not for some time. In the meantime, could you bear to keep an eye on it for me? Use it, if you wish, as a little refuge. You helped to turn it into the charming place it is, I should like you to enjoy it for a while.

We'll meet again before too long. Once again, thank you for some precious weeks and warm memories.

Roderick Landry xx

Two kisses. With the tip of a finger, she stroked the crosses after his name.

How long she lay back in the chair with the letter held close against her heart, she didn't know. When at last she stood up, her legs felt stiff. She shivered.

It was beginning to get chilly as the sun went in and rain clouds began to gather over the sea. The waves, reflecting the sky above, had the stillness of an impending storm.

She let herself out of the house and carefully closed the door. She'd need to hurry if she was to reach home before the rain started.

As she walked, she scolded herself severely. Don't get into a state. Roderick had promised nothing. Any love was purely on her side. She would wait for him to return — he'd promised that — then they would see.

In the meantime, she'd look after the cottage. Johnny and Isaac would help her keep the garden in good shape and she would tackle the kitchen. She'd make a list of what was needed and take a few trips into nearby towns to collect the items. She was not going to pine!

By now she had reached the bottom of the hill that led up to the hotel. On the low wall at the end of the lane that led to the Perrans' cottage, was the one person she didn't want to see.

'Hello, Elf,' said Jack. He had the grace to look shamefaced.

Reluctantly, she stopped. 'How's your leg?'

'Getting better.' He indicated the crutches at his feet. 'I can get around. Never mind me, how are you?' He studied her face. 'You look as if you've been crying.'

She rubbed at her eyes. 'It's the wind. I've been walking near the sea.' She was about to say goodbye and hurry on when the first huge spots of rain began to fall.

Jack reached for his crutches and clumsily positioned them under his arms. 'Come on, young Elf, you can't get home in time. Come down to our place. Mam will make you a drink. Nancy's there.'

That decided her. She wanted to see Nancy. They hurried as fast as Jack could move down the lane to the little whitewashed cottage.

Mrs Perrans was in her usual seat in the kitchen with Nancy nearby. The girl jumped up when she saw her friend.

'Elf. What's wrong. Are you all right?'

Elvina was startled. Her sadness must show in her face more than she realised.

'I'm very well,' she said, forcing a smile. 'How are you, Mrs Perrans?'

Nancy's mother squeezed her hand and motioned for her to take Nancy's place. Then she sent Nancy to make them all a cup of tea.

Mrs Perrans started straight away to talk about the subject which was on all their minds.

'I've been hearing about last night,' she said. She gave her son a severe look. 'I'm ashamed of our Jack.'

Jack began to speak but his mother held up a hand. 'It's no good arguing, you spoilt the evening for everyone. And to behave like that to Elvina's friend. We owe him a lot. Look how he helped Johnny and Daisy. I'm ashamed of you.'

'Oh, Mam,' protested Jack, wriggling with embarrassment.

'What did Mr Landry say?' she asked Elvina. 'Is he still mad? I heard he went back to the hotel on his own.'

'Mr Landry's gone,' said Elvina quietly. 'I haven't spoken to him since the dance.'

'Gone?' Nancy placed a cup of tea in front of her. 'You mean back to where he came from?'

Elvina nodded, not trusting herself to speak.

'There!' said Mrs Perrans, glaring at Jack again.

'Oh, Elf.' Nancy sat beside her and put a hand on her arm.

Elvina tried to smile. 'Don't worry about me, Nan, There was nothing between us — only friendship.'

Nancy looked doubtful. 'You say you haven't spoken to him?'

'He left me a letter at the cottage. I'm going to look after it while he's away.

I'll ask Johnny and Isaac if they'll keep an eye on the garden. I'll have to pay them in gobstoppers, I expect.' She gave a little laugh which turned into a sob. Nancy put an arm round her shoulders.

Elvina recovered herself. 'He's coming back,' she said, with forced brightness. 'He's made plans for a garage business in the Midlands. They'll take up a lot of his time. When he's not busy, he'll be back.'

'So he won't sell the cottage?' asked Mrs Perrans.

'Not for a while. I can use it if I like. I have a key.'

Mrs Perrans poured them all another cup of tea. 'Try one of these,' said Nancy, offering a plate. 'Eli's been experimenting with biscuits — these are lemon — so I brought some for Mother to try.'

As she tasted the biscuit, Elvina saw Nancy give her mother a quick glance. Mrs Perrans nodded.

Nancy took Elvina's hands. 'I've got

something to tell you,' she said, colouring a little.

Jack heaved himself to his feet. 'If you're talking women's chat, I'm off. It's stopped raining. I'll see you later, Elf.'

They heard the front door slam. 'We're very sorry about everything,' said Mrs Perrans. 'He's a good lad but thing's aren't going too well for him at the moment.'

'You mean his leg. Well that was his own fault.'

'I know, my love,' said the older woman. 'I'm not making excuses for him but he's always loved you, even as a child, and he can't accept that you could love anyone else. It's not your fault.'

'I feel dreadful about it,' Elvina admitted, 'but you can't force yourself to love someone. Jack has always been a dear friend, I hope he always will be when he's got over this . . .' she fluttered her fingers uncertainly.

'He's making some plans,' Mrs

Perrans confided. 'I can't say what they are, he'll tell you himself. I'm not happy about them, but perhaps they'll be the answer to his problems.' She took a biscuit. 'Now then, Nan, tell Elvina your news.'

Nancy had been sitting quietly during this exchange, but as Elvina looked at her, she could see that her friend was holding something in with great difficulty. Suddenly, she realised what it was.

'Nancy! Are you . . . are you . . . ?'

Nancy nodded vigorously. 'You've guessed. Yes, I'm going to have a baby!'

Elvina, her problems forgotten for the moment, flung her arms round the other girl. 'Oh Nan, how lovely! When? Do you want a boy or a girl? What does Eli think? Of course, he's over the moon.'

Nancy laughed. 'Slow down. You're as excited as me. Eli's thrilled — it's what he wanted — a son to take over the business. We can have a girl later.'

Mrs Perrans chuckled. 'You can't

order them like that, my girl.'

Elvina gave a little sigh and leaned back on her chair. 'It's wonderful news. A baby. Have you thought of some names?'

Nancy gave her a shy smile. 'Well, as you'll be the chief godparent . . . '

'Oh, Nan, will I really?'

'Of course. As you'll be the chief godparent,' she repeated, 'we're going to call him Elvin.'

Elvina's eyes filled with tears. 'I think I'm going to cry. Little Elvin. I can't wait to hold him.'

'You'll have to wait quite a time,' observed Mrs Perrans, 'Nancy's only just found out.'

There was silence for a few minutes, each woman busy with her own thoughts, then Elvina glanced at the window. 'Yes, it's stopped raining. I must get back. Wait till I tell the aunts, they'll be excited too.'

She kissed Nancy and Mrs Perrans and hurried out. The aunts would be pleased she had something else to occupy her thoughts.

She turned in at the gate of the hotel and jumped as a man stepped out of the bushes.

'Hello, Elf.'

'Jack! You gave me a fright. What are you doing hiding there?'

'I didn't want the aunts to see me. I don't expect they like me very much now.'

'Don't be silly. Of course they like you. They just think you've behaved very badly lately.'

'And you think that too? He looked at her but she made no reply.

'You're right. I've been doing a lot of thinking while I haven't been able to work. Just because we've always been friends, it doesn't follow that we'll — you know — fall in love and get married,' he said with obvious embarrassment.

Still Elvina made no answer.

'Elf, will you give me a definite answer to something? An answer that means you'll never change your mind?

Because if I think you might change your mind some day, that there's hope . . . '

'Jack,' she said gently, knowing what he wanted to ask, 'you're my best friend, after Nancy. I shall always want you as a best friend, but if you're asking whether I'll marry you, I'm afraid the answer is no and always will be.'

Jack stared at the ground as if trying to make up his mind about something, Then he said, 'I've been making plans for if you refused me. Well you have, so I'll tell you. Me and some of the lads have decided to leave here.'

'Leave here? Why? Where will you go?'

'America.'

'America! Jack, you can't. We'll never see you again.'

'You will, if I make my fortune,' he said with a grin.

'But . . . America! Do you have to go quite so far away? What about your mother?'

'She's got the others,' he said. 'And

maybe I'll help her better by sending money home. Lots of lads from Cornwall have gone to America for a better life. Land of opportunities, they call it.'

Elvina felt stunned. This was turning out to be a day of shocks. First Roderick, then Nancy's news, now Jack. She felt she wanted to sit down.

'Jack, come inside and we can talk there.'

'No.' He turned towards the gate. 'There's no more to say at the moment. We're just making plans. I'll let you know when I know more myself.'

'But Clay. What about Clay?'

'Clay wants to make his fortune too,' he said with a grin, 'but he wants me to try first. When I've been out there for a year or two, he'll join me.'

'But what will you do in America?'

'Don't know yet. They have fisher-men there. P'raps I'll carry on with my old job. Or p'raps I'll be one of those film stars. That'd please our Daisy.' Whistling to himself, he swung away down the road on his crutches.

Elvina watched him go. Dear Jack, perhaps a new life would be the best idea for him.

Thoughtfully, she made her way round to the kitchen door of the hotel. Her aunts looked up as she entered. Their expressions were concerned.

They're wondering what I've been doing, and whether I've got any news of Roderick, she thought.

She removed her hat and sat down at the table. 'If you've an hour to spare,' she said, 'I'll tell you about my day.'

Elvina Still Pines
For Roderick

Elvina kept herself busy for the next two weeks, making lists at the cottage and excursions into nearby towns to buy items for the kitchen. She bought knives and saucepans, a flat iron and some clothes pegs and three fancy brass jelly moulds to add a gleam to the shelf above the range.

She went to the cottage every afternoon when she had finished her chores at the hotel. The aunts knew where she was going but made no comment. She didn't like being secretive but she couldn't discuss what she was doing.

Nancy was too engrossed in preparations for her baby to wonder what her friend was doing. Daisy offered to go for a walk with her, but Elvina replied that she was too busy at the moment. Daisy caught the little frown on Aunt Susie's face and wandered off.

Being at the cottage gave Elvina both joy and agony. She was in Roderick's house where he had spent so much time over the last few months. She was touching his belongings, sitting in the chair he'd bought her, cleaning and polishing until every surface shone, as if he would come back at any moment.

But he wasn't there and she daren't contemplate the thought that he might never come back.

Very little mail was delivered at Spindrift Cottage, but whenever there was a letter, she picked it up with a sharp intake of fear in her stomach. What if he wrote to say he was selling the cottage?

But that particular letter never came. One day there was an envelope addressed to her. Nervously, she opened it to find a birthday card. It was signed, *With love, Roderick*. As on the letter, there were two kisses.

'With love,' she read aloud. Did that mean anything or was it just a formality? Again, she touched the kisses with the tip of a finger. Now she had four kisses. Did that add up to anything?

She placed the card on top of a small cupboard near her chair, where she could see it, and walked across to the window. She stood motionless, looking out at the waves. Cornwall with all its beauty meant everything to her, but if Roderick asked her to leave and go up-country with him, she'd go without a backward glance at the sea and the sand.

Feeling like a traitor, but defiant, she went out into the garden. Weeds were beginning to spring up. She pulled up a few, then decided to see Johnny about the garden on the way home.

The next day, she and Johnny and Isaac worked all the afternoon in the garden, weeding, sweeping and burning. It was a Saturday and the boys were free all day.

'Make sure we finish before the shop closes,' said Johnny. 'You said you'd pay us in gobstoppers, don't forget.'

'You and your gobstoppers,' said Elvina with a laugh.

'When's Mr Landry coming back?' asked Isaac.

Elvina bent over a border and forked furiously until she thought her voice would be steady. 'I'm not sure,' she said at last. 'He had a lot of business to attend to at home.'

'Isn't this his home?'

'No. He lives in the middle of England, a long way from here.'

'He's going to open a garage,' said Johnny, importantly. 'Clay told me.'

'P'raps he'll never come back here,' said Isaac.

'Why don't we stop now,' Elvina suggested. 'We've worked so hard and the garden looks wonderful.'

In the village, she took the boys to the sweet shop and handed over some money to the shopkeeper. She left them all discussing the rival merits of gobstoppers and treacle toffee.

Outside the garage, she bumped into Clay. He gave her a sheepish grin which, for the moment, puzzled her. But his first words explained it.

'Elf, I must tell you before someone else does. I've been out with a girl a few times lately.'

She found it hard not to smile at the expression on his face. 'Have you, Clay? That's very nice. Who is she?' She felt sure she knew the answer.

He ignored the question. 'Are you sure you don't mind?'

'No, Clay. I really don't mind. Who is she?'

'Jill Evans. You saw me dancing with her at the Festival dance.'

'I did. You seemed to be enjoying yourselves. You were doing some very fancy steps.'

He blushed. 'She's been teaching me. She's a good dancer.'

Elvina couldn't resist some gentle teasing. 'So you're getting very friendly?' she suggested.

'She says she likes me a lot,' he admitted, his blush deepening.

'And you like her?'

'Oh yes.' He spoke quickly then gave Elvina a guilty look. 'Not as much as I like you,' of course.

'Oh, Clay, I'm pleased you've found someone. We'll still be friends, of course, but you must find a girl of your own.'

'Jack told me what he asked you.'

'And did he tell you what I answered?'

'Yes.' He looked down at the ground. 'If I asked you the same question, what would you say?'

She put a hand on his arm. 'The same as I said to Jack. You're both my very best, my oldest friends, except for Nancy, but I will never marry either of you.'

His sigh was almost one of relief, she thought. Perhaps he was glad to know that that aspect of their lives was behind them. Now they could be friends with no thought of anything more.

'It's Roderick Landry, isn't it?' he asked, with no rancour in the question.

She paused before replying, then nodded. 'But he's gone away and I don't know when — or if — he'll be back.'

'He'll be back,' said Clay firmly. 'No one could leave a girl like you, Elf.'

Elvina swallowed the lump that had appeared in her throat.

★   ★   ★

In her bedroom that night, Elvina wondered what was to become of her. Was her life just to return to the quiet, uneventful way it had gone on before Roderick Landry arrived.

She'd lost all her best friends. Nancy was now a wife and almost a mother. Jack was preparing to travel to the other side of the world. Clay might follow him and in the meantime, had found himself a sweetheart.

And I have nothing, she told herself. She sat at her open window staring out across the sea, self-pity washing over her.

Then a picture came into her mind of the young men Roderick had described, the young soldiers who'd died in the mud and squalor of the trenches. They had no life at all now. They'd gone to France prepared to fight for their country, and had died there. She felt disgust for her self-pity.

She jumped up and closed the window. Then she stood in front of the mirror and looked at her reflection. 'Elvina Simmons, I'm ashamed of you,' she said out loud. 'You're just a grizzler. What would Roderick think if he could hear you?'

I have my health; two aunts who love me; a comfortable home and a brooch worth a great deal of money. Above all, I'm alive. Roderick will be back soon, I know he will. And then I shall have love too.

With that, she blew out her candle, turned onto her side and was soon asleep.

She slept soundly and awoke next morning refreshed, and in a quite different frame of mind. The day was beautiful with the light sun and crisp freshness of early autumn. Elvina decided to take some flowers down to Spindrift Cottage to brighten the living room.

'I forgot to buy a flower vase for the cottage,' she said to Aunt Susie. 'Do you have one I could borrow?'

Aunt Susie sorted through some vases in the china cupboard and produced three for Elvina's inspection.

'That one, please.' The girl picked out a white vase with a pattern of blue flowers on the side. 'I want some bright yellow flowers to make the room look sunny. Sometimes it looks quite dark.'

'The lilies are bright and tall enough for this vase,' said Aunt Susie. 'Pick some of those.'

'But they're your special flowers,' Elvina protested. 'I can't pick those.'

'I can spare a few in a good cause,'

said her aunt, with a smile. 'Pick what you need.'

The garden had a large bed of lilies, Aunt Susie's favourite flowers. Elvina picked a bunch and wrapped them carefully in paper. Then with the vase in a bag, she made her way through the village to Spindrift Cottage.

She filled the vase with water and placed it on the windowsill overlooking the beach. Then she arranged the flowers and stood back to admire the effect. They seemed to reflect the sun's brightness and pass it into the room. They look like a beacon showing lost sailors the way home, she thought.

But the wandering traveller who came to the door was not a lost sailor. She spun round in alarm as a key rattled in the lock. The door was pushed open and Roderick stood there.

For what seemed an age they gazed at each other across the room. Elvina wanted to run to him but she couldn't move. He remained in the doorway looking at her.

Then he opened his arms and before she realised it, Elvina had crossed the room and was enfolded in his embrace.

'My little Elvina,' he whispered. 'I thought I could go away and work out my future with no thought of you. But I was wrong.' He bent and kissed her upturned face. 'I missed you so dreadfully, my darling. I couldn't work, I couldn't concentrate. I kept thinking of you.'

'Oh Roderick, I knew you'd come back,' she whispered.

'I'm back and I shall never leave again without you,' he said, giving her another kiss.

He closed the door and holding her closely, took her to the couch. 'Let's be comfortable, my love,' he said. 'We have so much to talk about.'

'When did you decide to come back?' she asked.

'Yesterday. I packed a bag and drove through the night. I couldn't bear to wait any longer. I had to see you.'

She lifted a hand to his face and

stroked his cheek. 'I knew you would come and yet I can't believe you're here.'

'My little love,' he whispered, holding her tightly and kissing her hair.

'What about your garage?' she asked.

'That's progressing well, mostly thanks to Ralph. He's worked so hard. He found us just the right premises, near to the city but not in it. We shan't be opening for several weeks yet.'

'And what about . . . ' Elvina began, but he closed her mouth with his lips. After a moment he said, 'Do you really want to talk business? I came all this way to hold you and to tell you that I love you. I don't want to talk about garages — not now anyway.'

'Do you really?' she asked, wonderingly.

'Do I really what?'

'Do you really love me?'

'My dear girl, haven't I just said so.'

'Oh Roderick, I dreamed that one day you'd say that. But I thought you'd find someone more sensible than me once you went away.'

'Sensible! Why should I want a sensible girl? I can be sensible enough for both of us. I want my bright, happy, cheerful little Elvina. Now give me a kiss and tell me that you love me too.' He looked deep into her eyes and she felt a shiver down her spine.

For a moment Kitty Rawlings came into her mind. She pushed it aside.

'No one will ever love you as much as I do,' she said fiercely. 'No one.'

For a moment he looked startled, then he smiled. 'If you feel like that,' he said, 'I have something important to ask you.' Before she could speak, he had slipped to his knees before her.

'Elvina, I love you,' he said. 'Will you marry me?'

For a moment she couldn't speak, then she flung her arms around him. 'Yes, yes, yes, of course I will.'

He reached into his pocket and brought out a small blue box. Inside, on a bed of blue velvet lay an exquisite ring of five sparkling diamonds. Elvina gazed at it in rapture.

'I hope you like it,' he said, anxiously. 'I don't know what you really like but I wanted to bring you a ring so that you couldn't change your mind.'

'Change my mind,' she said with a laugh, holding out her hand. He slipped the ring onto her finger and gave it a kiss.

'There, now you're mine.'

They sat, unspeaking, hands entwined, for a long time. Then Elvina whispered, 'I don't think I've ever been so happy.'

He sat up and turned to look at her. 'I shall make sure that you are always happy,' he said. 'But there is a problem.'

'A problem?' she looked worried.

'You belong here. You've always said you'd hate to leave. But my business is far away from the sea. Could you be happy there?'

'I'll be happy wherever you are,' she said. 'And we have our dear little Spindrift Cottage. We can come back often, can't we?'

'As often as you wish.'

She noticed something he'd placed

just inside the door when he arrived.

'You've brought your painting equipment. Does that mean . . . ?'

'I told myself that if you accepted me, I'd paint again,' he said.

'So the horrid memories of the war have gone?'

'No, they'll never go. But they are not as dreadful. I can live with them. They are a part of my past life. This is the present. I have you and I shall paint.'

He set up his easel facing the window and took out his palette. 'The flowers framed by the window with the beach and the sea beyond,' he said. 'I'll paint it and we'll hang it on the wall in our home in Worcestershire where it will always remind you of Cornwall.'

'What a lovely idea.' Elvina perched on a little stool beside him and watched as he skilfully applied paint to canvas. Before her eyes, the scene appeared; her flowers in their blue and white pot with the beach behind, foam-edged waves and the blue and white sky.

He smiled down at her as he worked.

She watched the quick, skilful movements of his brush.

'You paint quickly.'

'I learned that in the army. There was no time to consider the scene, I had to get an impression as quickly as possible. He worked in silence for a few minutes.

Suddenly Elvina put up a hand. 'Stop. Wait a minute.' She opened her bag and took out an envelope. Extracting the letter inside, she placed it on the windowsill with the envelope nearby.

He looked from the letter to the girl beside him 'Is that the letter . . . ?'

'The letter you left for me? Yes. The letter that said you would be back. I read it here, but I've carried it everywhere with me since that day. It's the finishing touch for the picture.'

He bent and kissed the top of her head. 'It is. And it will remind me of how we parted and how I just had to come back.'

★ ★ ★

Two hours later, Roderick threw down his brush. 'Finished!' He drew his hand across his face. 'Phew! Quite a marathon.'

Elvina gazed at the picture. The windows, half open, framed the vase of flowers. Behind them, footprints crossed the sand and led down to the calm blue sea edged with little rocks and curling foam. On the wooden window sill lay a crumpled letter while above the window, a few soft fronds of greenery trailed downwards.

The painting perfectly captured the scene in front of them. Now they could never forget the day Roderick returned to Spindrift Cottage and asked Elvina to be his wife.

Elvina had never seen her aunts so quietly excited as when she returned to the hotel holding Roderick's hand, and wearing her beautiful diamond ring.

Roderick, standing behind her, looked a little shamefaced. 'I should have asked you first, I know,' he said, 'but I couldn't wait. Elvina might have decided not to accept me if I'd given her time to think.'

They all laughed when Elvina said, 'If he hadn't asked me, I think I should have asked him.'

'We're delighted with your news,' said Aunt Tilly. 'When do you plan to be married?'

'We haven't made any plans,' said Elvina. 'Roderick has been painting ever since he got back.'

'Painting,' repeated Aunt Susie. 'I thought the cottage was finished.'

Roderick and Elvina laughed delightedly. 'Not painting the cottage, painting a picture,' Elvina explained. 'We'll show you when it's dry.'

'So you're painting again,' said Aunt Tilly. 'I'm glad. You should never neglect a talent.'

'And what about your business?' asked Aunt Susie. 'It's a long way from here, isn't it?'

'That's the only problem. I'm afraid I shall be taking your niece away to live in the Midlands.'

'Oh!' Aunt Susie sat down suddenly.

'I hadn't thought of that.'

Elvina crossed to her aunt and took her hand. 'Don't be upset about it, not when I'm so happy. We shall come back often, and you can come and stay with us when the season is quiet.'

Aunt Susie patted her hand. 'Of course we shall. And we always knew that you would leave us some time.'

Aunt Tilly fetched a bottle of wine and some glasses. 'I think we should have a toast,' she said. 'To Elvina and Roderick.'

'May they always be as happy as they are today,' said Aunt Susie.

★ ★ ★

After Nancy's small quiet wedding and Daisy's informal, exuberant village one, Elvina was afraid hers might be an anticlimax.

But she need not have worried. It combined the best elements of both the other weddings.

Her dress was as beautiful as that

worn by Nancy. She and Aunt Susie had visited the best bridal shop in Truro and carried the dress home in triumph.

The centre panel of the cream satin skirt was lavishly embroidered with flowers and beads and the skirt swept into a small train behind her. Her lace veil, secured by a circlet of cream flowers, sat low on her forehead in the fashionable mode.

Roderick, handsome in his army uniform, caused quite a flutter amongst the women waiting around the church door for the happy couple to emerge. Ralph, his best man, was also in uniform.

Ralph had given them a very unusual present. He had asked his aunt and uncle if they would allow the reception to be held at Penhallow Hall. Lady Crace was delighted to be asked. The Hall had not hosted a wedding for twenty years. She busied herself chivvying the gardeners into providing the most spectacular flowers for decorations.

Elvina's aunts had expected to prepare everything at the hotel, but Roderick had insisted on the Hall.

'You must have a rest,' he told them. 'You are very special guests. We want you to enjoy the day.'

The Hall made a splendid background for the photographs. Elvina, with her bridesmaids, Annie and Jill, in dresses of palest blue, posed in the autumn sunshine. She'd wanted Nancy to be her matron of honour, but Nancy had refused. She was not having an easy pregnancy and preferred to rest and watch the proceedings.

In the evening, the villagers, nervous and dressed in their Sunday best, came to the Hall. But nervousness was forgotten when the fiddlers struck up a tune for dancing and Elvina and Roderick joined in the fun.

After an hour, the happy couple made their way to the table where Roderick's parents were sitting with Aunt Susie and Aunt Tilly.

'We're going to creep away now,' said

Roderick. 'We've come to say goodbye.'

Of course, creeping away was impossible. They were spotted and a large crowd waited on the steps to wave them off.

Elvina, in a cream suit and tiny blue hat, stood up in the car to throw her bouquet. A laughing Jill caught it.

'She'll marry Clay and go to America with him, I expect,' said Elvina with satisfaction.

'Never mind matchmaking,' said Roderick with a fond smile, 'sit down and we'll be off.'

Elvina tied a soft blue scarf over her hat and Roderick tucked a rug around her knees.

'Ready, Mrs Landry?' he asked.

'Yes, Mr Landry,' she said demurely. To shouts and applause, they set off down the long drive of Penhallow Hall.

Three hours later, they descended the steps of their honeymoon hotel, and wandered arm in arm through the evening-scented gardens to the seashore. The moon had risen just above the horizon and cast a beam like a golden path across the sea to the beach.

'Is there anywhere more magical than Cornwall?' asked Elvina, dreamily.

'Are you sure you can bear to leave it?'

Elvina turned towards him and wound her arms about his neck. 'I must leave because I must be with you,' she said simply, 'but we'll be back.'

He bent and kissed her lips. 'Of course,' he said. 'We'll return.'

THE END

We do hope that you have enjoyed reading this large print book.

Did you know that all of our titles are available for purchase?

We publish a wide range of high quality large print books including:
Romances, Mysteries, Classics
General Fiction
Non Fiction and Westerns

Special interest titles available in large print are:
The Little Oxford Dictionary
Music Book, Song Book
Hymn Book, Service Book

Also available from us courtesy of Oxford University Press:
Young Readers' Dictionary
(large print edition)
Young Readers' Thesaurus
(large print edition)

For further information or a free brochure, please contact us at:
Ulverscroft Large Print Books Ltd.,
The Green, Bradgate Road, Anstey,
Leicester, LE7 7FU, England.
Tel: (00 44) 0116 236 4325
Fax: (00 44) 0116 234 0205

FOLLOW YOUR HEART

Margaret Mounsdon

Marie Stanford's life is turned upside down when she is asked to house sit for her mysterious Aunt Angela, who has purchased a converted barn property in the Cotswolds. Nothing is as it seems . . . Who is the mysterious Jed Soames and why is he so interested in Maynard's? And can she trust Pierre Dubois, Aunt Angela's stepson? Until Marie can find the answers to these questions she dare not let herself follow her heart.